W9-AWJ-742

THE HANGING OF FATHER MIGUEL

nAvh
The Production Review Committee of N.A.V.H.
has found this book to meet its criteria
for large type publications.

THE HANGING OF FATHER MIGUEL

M.A. ARMEN

Thorndike Press • Thorndike, Maine

Library of Congress Cataloging in Publication Data:

Armen, M. A.
The hanging of Father Miguel / M. A. Armen.
p. cm.
ISBN 1-56054-008-7 (alk. paper : lg. print)
1. Large type books. I. Title.
[PS3551.R464H36 1990] 90-35641
813'.54--dc20 CIP

Thorndike Press Large Print edition published in 1990 by arrangement with M. Evans & Company, Inc.

Cover design by James B. Murray.

This book is printed on acid-free, high opacity paper.

For Garo, with love
and remembrances.

Prologue

The small adobe mission, a weathered leftover from the past, rose above the mesquite and cacti of the deserted plain. Shrouded in silence and isolation, it was a forgotten place – an eerie, decaying shelter for memories, dusty relics, and the bleak whispering of the wind.

In the shadow of its courtyard wall, an elderly Mexican, stoop-shouldered and frail, stood shading his eyes, squinting toward a late-model station wagon as it approached along the rutted, dirt access road. Wearing a faded, much-mended priest's robe, leaning on a vintage wooden cane, the old man seemed as much a specter from the past as the mission.

He remained motionless as the car stopped, a growing air of excitement in his manner as its only occupant alighted.

The visitor was in his early thirties, a gray-eyed man in a well-tailored western suit, his face shadowed by the brim of an expensive Stetson. As he glanced around curiously, the old priest stepped toward him, smiling gently.

"Welcome to Mission Miguel, sir. Visitors here are a rare treat." The quavery voice suggested that of a scholar.

The man in the Stetson looked up in surprise, aware of the priest for the first time. "Thank you. I heard there was an old mission here, but I thought it was abandoned."

"Only by the present. The past *still* shelters here."

The newcomer studied him, intrigued by the contrast between his shabby attire and his cultured speech.

"You mean memories of the past."

An enigmatic smile crossed the priest's face. "There is much more than memory here, sir. You see, the mission has been converted to a museum. It houses many rare and ancient relics."

The man looked off across the sun-baked loneliness of the surrounding plain. "Strange place for a museum – or even for a mission."

"Two centuries ago there was need for it in this place. It was erected by a little-known sect of Spanish priests as a haven for frontier wanderers, and for a small tribe of Indians who lived in the nearby hills."

The visitor's eyes lighted with interest. "What tribe?"

The old priest shrugged sadly. "Who can be sure? Their artifacts indicate that they were

Yaqui, but they themselves have long since disappeared."

"Didn't the priests here keep records?"

"Yes, but they, too, were consumed by time." The old man pointed toward a distant cluster of decaying buildings, the remains of a ghost town. "That place was known as Rileyville. The mission once served its inhabitants also." He sighed. "But they vanished into the past, just as the Indians did."

The visitor nodded. "I passed through it on my way here. Looks like it must've been quite a town."

"It was. Many interesting things occurred there."

The visitor was obviously intrigued. "All right if I look around?"

The old priest's face lighted eagerly. "By all means. Come, I will be your guide."

As they approached the courtyard, the visitor paused, his attention caught by a tarnished metal placard swinging from the high arch above the gateway. Squinting, he read the words on the placard.

"On this spot, Father Miguel, the priest, was hanged." His stunned face showed disbelief. "A *priest* was hanged here!"

The caretaker nodded solemnly. "It is a matter of record. It has to do with 'Father Diablo.'. . ."

"Father *Devil?* Who was he?"

"The Indians called him a demon. They thought he haunted this place." A sudden wind stirred dust devils around them and set the placard swaying creakily on its rusty chain.

A slight chill touched the visitor. "That's a strange legend."

"Or perhaps it is a strange truth." A twinkle showed briefly in the old priest's eyes. "I will let you decide which one for yourself."

Guiding his guest to a shaded bench, he began to tell a startling story. . . .

One

It was 1864, the early morning of a chill, sunless day. A lonely male figure, broad-brimmed hat pulled low, collar turned up against the cold, rode slowly across a desolate expanse of Arizona plain toward a bleak frontier town. He was the only moving thing between earth and sky.

Lean and hard-muscled, his eyes crow-tracked at the corners and piercing as a brace of Bowie knives, he slouched loose-hipped in the saddle, man and horse one movement. A Frontier Colt slapped his thigh, its slickened butt testifying to frequent use. He was still young, barely past his early thirties, but he had the look of a man who has come a far, hard way and doesn't want to go back.

He glanced up, saw that he was approaching the edge of the town, and lifted his horse to a jog, a gleam of anticipation easing the weariness of his face. Glint McClain had been gone from this place a long time, but now . . . now he was coming home. He entered the town, riding the middle of its almost deserted street, looking neither to right nor left, his thoughts on the small cabin a mile ahead, the cabin he had built with his own hands, for the woman who should be waiting for him there.

As McClain neared the saloon, a muscular stranger tying a scraggly mule to the hitch rail, studied him with sharp interest, his penetrating blue eyes in striking contrast to his strong Latin features.

Without seeming to, McClain noticed his scrutiny, saw that his dark buckskins and flat-crowned sombrero, both veiled with dust, were inscrutably plain and unadorned. A silver-handled sheath knife, fitted snugly against his back, was his only ornamentation. McClain noted, too, the man's arresting magnetism, decided he was more than just an idle drifter, and felt vaguely disturbed by his interest.

A slovenly, slack-jawed young cowpoke lounging near the batwings also noticed McClain. He straightened, eyeing horse and rider narrowly for an instant, then turned to the bartender who was sweeping the saloon steps.

"Hey, ain't that Glint McClain?"

The bartender glanced up impatiently, then froze, nodding strickenly.

Excitement flooded the cowpoke's face. "Whooee! Wait'll Hal Peters finds out!" Jerking his horse loose from the hitch rail, he pounded away, his shouts echoing along the street. "Glint McClain's back! Glint McClain's back!"

As he passed, the scattered handful of early risers looked after him, then each turned to stare uneasily toward the solitary rider continuing on toward the opposite edge of town.

The stranger noted their reactions thoughtfully, then finished tying his mule and ascended the saloon steps. He paused near the bartender, who had returned to his sweeping.

"Who is this Glint McClain?" His accent was traced with Spanish.

"Fast gun and a fast temper." The bartender's voice was gruff with uneasiness.

The stranger's blue eyes studied him shrewdly. "How fast?"

"Glint of steel. That's how he came by his name." The bartender turned back into the saloon.

The stranger looked after McClain for a moment, frowning thoughtfully. Then he turned and entered the saloon.

McClain rode steadily on. A short way beyond the town, he turned off the main road onto a rutted trail. He followed its winding path to the top of a small rise and reined in. A modest cabin stood in the meadow below. McClain saw, with a flood of warmth, that it was just as he remembered it – snugly built and sturdy. The curtains at its window were yellow muslin now instead of white, but the rosebush was still beside the door, the yard still neat and well tended.

Memories crowded his mind . . . the woman cutting roses, sitting with him before the crackling fireplace, humming as she worked at the stove. His throat tightened as he remembered the warmth of her body in the darkness, the smoothness of her breasts, the musky sweetness between her thighs. They'd shared so much together . . . everything but marriage and kids. Back then he wasn't sure enough to give her those . . . not sure he could stay put, keep his gun on the wall. Now he was.

McClain lifted the reins, squeezed his horse forward, his tired eyes alight with anticipation.

At the side of the cabin, a pretty young woman hung the last pair of faded overalls on the clothesline. As she picked up her empty wash basket, she heard the soft thud of approaching hooves. She walked to the corner of the cabin and looked toward the rise which ended a short distance from the front yard. Glint McClain had almost completed his descent.

The woman stared toward him disbelievingly for an instant, then terrified recognition engulfed her face. She whirled, raced toward the small barn behind the cabin. A man in stained coveralls was just emerging, a pail of milk in his hand. He stopped, startled by her expression.

"What's wrong, Em? What is it?"

"Glint McClain's here." Her voice was strangled. The man dropped the pail. Its contents spilled across the dirt, unnoticed. "He'll kill me sure!" His eyes were blind with fear.

She clutched his arm desperately. "Quick! He mustn't see you! Get the horse!" She hurried back toward the cabin yard as he scurried into the barn.

McClain dismounted near the door, started up the steps, then saw the woman coming toward him. She stopped as their eyes met, and he saw that she was taut and guarded.

"Em! Em, don't you know me?" He strode to her, his face warm, eager.

"Course I know you, Glint, course." She looked away from the hunger in his eyes. "But it's been so long. Nearly five years."

"I was fightin' for the Union."

"You was always fightin' somethin'."

"That's over now. I'm through with it. The fightin', the driftin'. Through with everything except you and this place."

She clenched her hands nervously. "You never wrote, never sent word, not since the day y'left." Her voice was tight, unsteady. "I thought you . . . you wasn't coming back."

"But you waited, Em. You still waited!" He reached for her ardently.

She backed away, fright clear on her face now. He saw it with surprise. "What is it, Em? What're you scared of?"

She shook her head, choking on words she couldn't say. Suddenly McClain noticed the clothesline, the wet overalls, the faded shirts. He crossed, tore a shirt from its place, and stared at it, rage slowly blackening his features.

She moved to him, desperate with terror. "Glint, I did wait . . . months, years!"

The fury pounding in his blood drowned her words. "Where is he?" He gripped her arm cruelly. *"Where?"*

From behind the cabin, the barn door creaked briefly. McClain tossed the shirt aside, strode toward the sound. She ran after him, clutching at him, shrieking.

"No, Glint! You gotta listen. Please! Please!"

McClain shook her off, kept walking. He rounded the cabin and saw the man in overalls near the open barn door. He was trying to mount a skittish workhorse.

McClain stopped, eyeing him coldly. "You won't be needin' the horse, fella."

The man stiffened, one foot in a stirrup. Then he eased to the ground and turned, ashen-faced, toward the gunfighter.

Stumbling, the woman thrust herself in

front of McClain. "Glint, we're *married!* I'm his *wife!*"

McClain's eyes wavered for an instant, then went hard again. "So now you'll be his widow." He thrust her aside roughly, returned his gaze to the man. "Get your gun."

"I'm a farmer, McClain, just a farmer. You'll be doin' murder!"

"Get your gun." McClain's voice was deadly.

The man fought to stop his trembling, leaned against the horse for support. Then he straightened slowly, summoning final, desperate courage.

"Gun won't save me, McClain." He met the gunfighter's gaze challengingly now, motioned toward the sobbing woman. "But killin' won't stop her lovin' me either."

The truth of his words hit McClain hard. He stared at the man, knowing he was right, knowing you could shoot away a life but not the feelings it had . . . the love or the tenderness, or even the hate and rage. No bullet could touch those. And they were what mattered, what counted between people. Once they were gone . . .

Slowly the anger drained from McClain's face, leaving it bleak and haggard.

"Forget it, farmer. I've had a bellyful of killin' anyhow." He turned away wearily, paused beside the woman, a terrible emptiness in his eyes. "Good luck, Em."

He walked stonily to the front of the cabin, mounted his horse, and jogged slowly away toward town.

Two

It was only midmorning, but the saloon was already crowded, its bar lined with a dusty assortment of leather-faced ranchers, wranglers, and farmers, its atmosphere charged with tension. Conversation stopped abruptly as McClain stepped through the batwings, and he knew at once that word of his return had spread.

Most of the faces turned toward him were familiar, but he saw no welcome in them. They held only the awareness of what he had been, and the dread of what he would bring back. McClain smiled bitterly. Fear had a long memory.

He crossed to the bar, returning the nervous greetings of those near him with a brusque nod. The line of men made room for him hastily. The bartender wiped a glass and set it in front of him.

"Whiskey, Glint?" The pleasantness in his tone was forced.

McClain nodded. "A double."

At a nearby table the stranger who rode the scraggly mule sat alone, a bottle of whiskey before him. He studied the gunfighter with the same sharp interest as before, sizing him up, taking his measure with odd intensity.

McClain drained his glass at a gulp, ordered a refill. As the bartender obliged, an Indian wearing the khaki of an army scout entered. He crossed unobtrusively to the bar and took the empty place next to McClain.

"Whiskey, please." The scout dropped a half-dollar on the counter.

The barkeep scowled at him. "Don't serve Injuns here. It's against the law."

"By army rules I'm the same as any trooper." The scout's quiet tones held undercurrents of irony.

"I told you – I don't *serve* Injuns."

McClain had listened to the exchange expressionlessly. Now he pulled a clean glass from the line on the inside edge of the bar. He turned it up, slid it in front of the scout.

"I'll serve him. Gimme the bottle."

The bartender hesitated uneasily. At his table the stranger's gaze sharpened. Suddenly he called out.

"Señor McClain!"

The gunfighter looked toward him.

"My compliments!" He tossed McClain his whiskey bottle.

McClain caught it, his eyes flicking the stranger briefly. *"Gracias."*

He turned back to the bar, filled the scout's glass, then raised his glance challengingly to the watching customers. They evaded his eyes uneasily. Nobody spoke.

McClain returned his attention to the Indian. "Drink up, soldier."

As they lifted their glasses, the batwings burst open and a tall, raunchy, mean-eyed kid of about twenty swaggered in. The young cowpoke who had first recognized McClain accompanied him.

The kid took in the scene at a glance. He called arrogantly, "Hold it, McClain!"

The other customers edged hastily to cover. Only the stranger at the table remained unmoving, his eyes alert and watchful.

McClain turned slowly to look at the kid, taking in the shiny Colt on his thigh, the well-oiled holster. His face remained unreadable as the kid crossed to confront him.

"I'm Hal Peters." The words were a challenge.

The saloon waited, tense and silent, for McClain's reply. It came flatly, after a long moment.

"So what's your beef?"

Peters glanced contemptuously at the army scout, spat at the man's feet. "I don't drink with

Injuns – no matter *who* says so."

For an instant McClain's eyes blazed, a muscle in his jaw twitching. Then his face went flat and expressionless. He shrugged. "They probably don't serve milk here, anyhow." The gunfighter drained his glass, tossed some coins on the bar, and started for the doors.

With a quick, lithe stride, the kid intercepted him. "I hear you're a fast gun, McClain. I say I'm faster!"

McClain met his narrow, brazen glance steadily. "I don't give a damn *what* you say." He brushed past the kid and disappeared through the batwings.

For a moment the room remained frozen, thrown off by the unexpected reaction. Then, cursing, Peters thrust his way outside. His companion and the rest of the saloon followed.

The stranger, a speculative frown on his face, remained seated until the room cleared. Then he rose, recovered his whiskey bottle from the bar, and moved casually after the others.

Crowded on the steps, the men watched in bewilderment as McClain's mounted figure galloped into the distance.

"Goddamn lily liver! He was scared t'draw on me!" Peters glanced around triumphantly. "Scared yellow!"

The barkeep shook his head. "No way, Peters. You just got lucky. Five years ago McClain would've killed ya!"

"Like hell he would!" Peters leaped angrily off the steps, swung aboard his horse, and dug in his spurs. The animal sprang away down the street, the other young cowpoke thundering after him.

As the crowd choked on their dust, the stranger shoved his whiskey bottle into the waiting mule's saddlebag, mounted, and jogged off in the direction taken by McClain. He was near the end of the street when the barkeep suddenly noticed him.

Startled, the barkeep darted into the saloon. He reappeared an instant later, shouting angrily.

"Hey! Hey – you on the jackass! Y' owe for the whiskey!"

The stranger continued on his way, the shouts either unheard or ignored.

With the town behind him, McClain slowed his horse to a jog and turned from the main trail to thread his way through a forest of towering boulders which jutted unexpectedly above the flat expanse of mesquite and scrub. The small stream was still there, just beyond the rocky maze. Nurtured by its moisture, several paloverdes shaded its rippling passage, their graceful limbs heavy with golden blossoms. They transformed the spot into a secret, sheltered oasis. In years past McClain had always watered here on his way to or from the town. It had invariably been deserted, showing no sign of other human use, and so he had come to regard it as his own – his private haven for rest and refreshment. He smiled bitterly, thinking that this was the only thing from his past which had remained the same, had held a welcome for his return.

He walked his horse into the water, dropped the reins, and sat waiting, allowing the thirsty animal to drink its fill. There was no sound except the rippling water and the soft, sucking noise the horse made. McClain's body responded to the tranquillity here, losing some of its weariness. He let his thoughts drift, pushing the aching memory of Em away determinedly, forcing himself to contemplate the future. He was alone with no one to care where he went or which trail he traveled. He realized that he didn't care much, either. Without somebody who needed him, the future didn't matter. All he wanted from it was peace – an absence of booming guns and blood and tattered banners and the cries of the dying. He'd wanted to share that future and its hope with Em. Now he just wanted to be left alone.

Suddenly his horse lifted its head, pricking its ears forward. It nickered questioningly toward the brush on the other side of the stream. An answering nicker brought McClain sharply out of his reverie. An instant later Hal Peters rode into view and halted, smirking at McClain across the slim margin of water.

"Figure t'hide out from me, McClain?"

McClain replied evenly, "Don't push your luck, kid."

The kid's blotchy face flushed angrily. "*You're* the one needs luck. Now git down an' draw or I'll shoot you outa the saddle."

McClain sighed wearily. "What's the matter? You tired of livin'?"

Peters motioned toward the silver coin which dangled from the gunfighter's neck, the outlines of a shamrock beaten into its surface. "I aim to have that lucky piece of yourn."

McClain's eyes went dangerous as broken glass. The coin was all he'd ever known of his father. He said flatly, "Lots of men wanted it."

"I'll count to three."

"Save your breath." McClain dismounted, moved away from his horse, and stood facing the kid, arms hanging loose, waiting.

The kid stepped carefully to the ground, backed up a few steps, his eyes steady on the gunfighter.

"Say when," said McClain.

"Now!" yelled the kid.

Streaking, their guns cleared leather and exploded into the silent, outraged air.

On the trail beyond the bouldered maze, the stranger on the mule heard the violent sound and halted. His startled gaze searched the tangled rocks for an instant. Then he urged the mule among them. As he rounded a boulder, Hal Peters came charging toward him, whooping triumphantly and waving McClain's lucky piece in the air.

He veered sharply around the stranger, shouting as he passed, "I shot Glint McClain! I shot Glint McClain!"

The stranger's blue eyes darkened with concern. He whipped the mule to a jog, zigzagged through the boulders until he reached McClain's horse. It stood ground-tied a short distance from the stream. McClain was crumpled at its feet, a bloodstain widening slowly across his shoulder and chest.

The stranger dismounted quickly, dropped down beside the fallen man, and lifted his head gently, feeling his neck for a pulse. The gunfighter's eyes opened. He stared up at the stranger, groggy recognition pushing through the glaze of pain.

"Don't need you. Need a priest." The words were slurred, barely audible.

The stranger fumbled in a pocket, drew out a rosary and held it for McClain to see. He said quietly, “I *am* a priest.”

Their eyes held for an instant, then McClain dropped into black unconsciousness.

Three

McClain wakened slowly and painfully. He saw that it was night, that he was looking at the stars through the screen of a crude mesquite awning which stretched above him. His shoulder and chest throbbed with a dull, hot ache that seemed to spread across his body like giant, clenching fingers. It brought back the memory of Hal Peters facing him across the stream, of the kid's gun erupting a split second before his own, of the searing agony as its bullet tore into him.

Alarm surged through McClain. Where was he? Who had brought him here, and why? As he fought to mend the torn strands of recollection, he became aware of heaviness against his wounds. He tried to lift his head, but he was too weak.

Forcing back the pain which movement brought, he inched his good arm upward and explored the heaviness with his fingers. Astonished, he realized that a poultice was bandaged tightly against his wound with leather thongs.

It brought back sudden memory of the stranger's face looking down at him. Hope flickered in his mind. He turned his head carefully.

Startled, he found himself staring at what appeared to be a large silver crucifix. It was only a few feet away, gleaming against the lights and shadows of a leaping fire. McClain blinked, struggled to orient. Suddenly his vision cleared and he saw the stranger bending over a small campfire. His back was to the gunfighter, and he was stirring something in a pot which hung above the flames. What McClain had thought was a crucifix was actually the silver handle of the sheath knife which hung at the stranger's waist.

McClain tried to elbow up, sank back with a moan as pain seared his shoulder and chest. The stranger turned, his face brightening as he saw that the gunfighter was fully conscious.

"Lie quietly or you will bleed again."

McClain nodded weakly, motioned toward the silver-handled knife. "Thought I was dead – that was a crucifix."

The stranger grinned, his teeth flashing whitely in the firelight. "For you it *was,* in a way."

"How do you figure?"

"The bullet in your body was deep. Without the knife's long blade, I could not have removed it."

McClain studied his swarthy face with a mixture of curiosity and puzzle. "Sure went to a lotta trouble for an hombre y'don't even know."

The stranger's blue eyes widened bewilderedly. "Don't *know?* But all men are brothers, my friend."

McClain eyed him narrowly, unable to decide whether he was faking or sincere. Suddenly a horse stomped in the nearby brush and nickered. McClain stiffened, alarm flooding his features.

The stranger reassured him quickly. "Rest easy. It is only your horse. He is tied at the stream with my own animal."

McClain glanced around, recognizing his surroundings for the first time, wondering why they had seemed so unfamiliar.

The stranger seemed to read his mind. "You were gravely hurt, my friend. You have been delirious for two days. That is why I could not move you from this place."

McClain stared at him, stunned. "I been layin' here *two* days – knowin' nothin'?"

The stranger nodded soberly. "I applied poultices and herbs to your wound. But it is only by the will of Heaven that you survived."

"Looks like the will of Heaven got a lotta help from you," replied McClain dryly.

The stranger shook his head, smiling. "It

is *I* who received help from Heaven, my friend."

"Anyhow, I'm obliged. I owe you, and I won't forget it." McClain's voice was gruffly sincere. He was unaccustomed to being helped, or to needing it.

Suddenly he remembered the moment when the stranger found him, the rosary dangling from his fingers. He asked sharply, "Before I passed out, didn't I hear you say you're a priest?"

"I am, indeed. My name is Father Miguel."

McClain eyed him skeptically, noting the sinewy strength of his body, the small knife scar on one cheek. "Sure don't look like much of a priest."

Miguel seemed amused. "What *do* I look like?"

McClain started to shrug, winced with pain. "Maybe a greaser *bandido* on the run."

Miguel grinned wickedly, jerked a finger toward McClain's poultice. "You don't look like much of a gunfighter, either."

Their eyes met and held. Then they burst into laughter, deciding they liked each other.

After a moment, McClain said ruefully, "I'm *not* much of a gunfighter anymore – lifted too many cannonballs in the army. Got arthritis in my fingers."

Disturbance rippled across Miguel's features.

"So that is why Hal Peters was able to shoot you!"

McClain nodded wryly. "Stiff hand slows your draw considerable."

Miguel was soberly thoughtful for a moment, then brightened. "But you still have your reputation. That is the main thing!"

McClain shook his head. His eyes turned brooding. "I'm through with gunfighting. War killed my taste for it. There's better ways t'settle things."

Miguel nodded sympathetically. "During the fever, you told much about your suffering in the army – the many battles you fought."

"How much?" Suspicion sharpened McClain's voice.

Miguel met his hard look and replied quietly, "I know you are a deserter."

"Figure on turnin' me in? That why you doctored me?"

The notion seemed to interest Miguel. "How much is the reward?"

"Enough t'buy whiskey." McClain's eyes were granite now.

The priest considered for an instant, then shook his head. "It is against my vows to reveal a confession." He grinned. "And anyway, I have whiskey." He crossed to where his saddlebags lay, pulled out the bottle he had taken from the saloon, and extended it to McClain.

McClain took it, the doubt on his face becoming amusement. "*Gracias* again."

The words brought a sudden cloud to Miguel's features. "It is the saloon owner who should be thanked. In the excitement, I forgot to pay him."

"*Forgot?*"

Miguel nodded unhappily. "It is a terrible thing, I know. But it is true."

"Why didn't you go back?"

"And leave you to die? Heaven would never forgive me!"

McClain studied the priest's shocked face suspiciously, again unable to decide whether he was faking or sincere. At last he shook his head, giving up the puzzle, tilted the bottle, and drank.

More than a week had passed, but Hal Peters still boasted about his shoot-out with Glint McClain. Lounging against the bar, the gunfighter's lucky piece dangling from his neck, he repeated the story for everybody in the saloon who would listen.

"I tell ya, when he got off his horse, he was shakin' like a leaf. Didn't wanna draw on me for nothin'!"

"I knew McClain a long time, kid. Never once saw him run scared." The challenge came from a leather-faced waddy with a score of saddle years behind him.

Peters glowered at him. "I shot him, I tell ya!" He jerked a finger at the lucky piece. "This here's the proof!"

Another taunt came from somewhere at the far end of the bar. "You coulda *found* that, Peters."

The leather-laced waddy agreed coldly. "That's for sure, Peters."

The kid stepped away from the bar and scanned the line of skeptical faces hotly. "You don't believe me, go take a look at the body. It's layin' right by the stream."

There was a small silence. Then the waddy drawled casually, "Might just mosey out an' do that, kid." He paid for his whiskey and crossed toward the batwings.

With over a week of rest behind him, McClain was fast regaining his strength. His wound had closed rapidly – a tribute to his basic good health and, according to Miguel, the benevolence of Heaven. The two men sat beside the little stream near their camp, McClain with his wounded arm in a tattered sling fashioned from an old undershirt, Miguel whittling on a stick with his silver-handled knife. They were lazily relaxed, enjoying the pleasantly warm day, the gentle breeze which stirred the paloverde trees and sent their golden blossoms to drift across the water. A casual intimacy had sprung up between them, but doubts about Miguel's veracity still lingered in McClain's mind.

"You sure can handle that knife." McClain was watching Miguel's whittling fingers idly. "Everything from stickin' fish to carvin' wood."

"A fine blade is a useful tool."

"A useful weapon, too." McClain was testing again, his words carefully deliberate.

Miguel looked up, shocked. "Weapon! I am a man of peace! It is against my vows to carry such a thing."

McClain gestured insistently toward the long, gleaming blade.

"Way I figure, a pigsticker like that's as good as a gun."

Miguel considered his words soberly for a moment, then brightened. "You have a point, my friend. But the answer is simple. In the hands of a fighter, a knife is a weapon. For a priest, it is only a tool!"

McClain frowned, trying to unravel his reasoning, thinking that, like most things about Miguel, it was a packet of contradictions and upside-down talk that some way turned out to make sense.

"You think like a pretzel," he grumbled. "There's a puzzle to everything about you."

Miguel seemed hurt. "How can a simple

priest be a puzzle?"

"What kinda priest goes wanderin' around saloons, drinkin' whiskey?"

"That is no puzzle. It is the practice of my order. We are required to subject ourselves to worldly temptations as a means of testing our virtue."

McClain snorted. "You expect me t'*believe* that?"

"True virtue must resist temptation, my friend. Not avoid it."

"Looked like you were doin' more drinkin' than resistin'."

Serenely, Miguel pointed out that drinking liquids was a natural thing. Only *drunkenness* was wrong. The priest added that he had obviously entered the saloon due to the will of God.

"The will of God! How do you figure that?" McClain was outraged.

"If I had not lingered there before continuing my journey, you would be dead now, McClain."

For an instant the gunfighter was speechless. Then he said in exasperation, "You've sure got a knack for figurin' the will of God!"

"That is part of my duty," said Miguel humbly.

As McClain scowled, still not totally convinced, the sound of approaching hoofbeats reached them faintly.

Both men tensed, coming to their feet, looking toward the sound. McClain said tightly, "Don't usually get company here."

"Perhaps Hal Peters became curious."

"I been thinkin' he might."

"So have I." Miguel's eyes met his, their depths reflecting the same dark apprehension. He added quietly, "It will be better if you are not seen, my friend."

He crossed quickly to McClain's horse, grabbed its halter rope, and gestured toward a thick island of marsh grass a short distance downstream.

"That growth – quickly! It will conceal you!" He shoved the halter rope into McClain's hand.

"What about you? If it's Peters . . ."

Miguel interrupted firmly, "You forget, McClain. I have the protection of Heaven." He shoved the gunfighter in the direction of the marsh grass and hurried up the bank toward the campsite.

The approaching hoofbeats were clear and definite now. McClain hesitated, listening to them, torn with conflicting emotions. Then, as if realizing that he had no choice, he waded downstream, pulling his horse behind him, making as little splash as possible.

When the newcomer jogged into view, Miguel was hunkered near the dead campfire, whetting his knife on a rock. He had adopted a sullen, recalcitrant look, and his dark sombrero was punched out of shape, pulled low on his forehead.

"Howdy." The leather-laced waddy from the saloon reined in and stepped to the ground.

"Buenos días." The priest's voice was different, too. It held the rough intonation of a peasant.

Listening from behind the marsh grass, McClain hardly recognized it. He parted the brush carefully, peered out as if to assure himself that the speaker was really Miguel.

"You savvy English?" asked the waddy.

Miguel didn't bother to look up. "I savvy."

The cowboy glanced around searchingly, poked briefly into the nearby brush. Miguel continued sharpening the knife, watching him from lidded eyes.

"How long you been camped here?"

"Five – maybe six days." Miguel gave the waddy a dark glance. "What you care, hombre?"

The man hesitated uncomfortably, then blurted, "Seen a dead body anyplace?"

"I have seen many dead bodies."

The waddy frowned uneasily, disturbed by his manner. "I mean here. Did y'see one here?"

Miguel rose slowly, still holding his knife.

"You look for a dead man *here?*" His tone held ominous undercurrents.

"That's right." The cowboy's uneasiness was increasing.

Miguel eyed him coldly for a moment, then pointed with his knife blade. "He was there. Right where you stand."

The cowboy moved hastily to another spot. "What happened to him? Y'bury him?"

Miguel shook his head, his piercing blue eyes impaling the man. "I didn't know he belonged to somebody."

"Belonged? What – what d'ya mean?"

Miguel wiped his knife blade on his thigh and moved slowly toward the cowboy. "I am a poor man. I have no money, no gun for hunting. . . ." He paused, hefted the knife casually. His voice turned soft as silk. "A man must eat – right, hombre?"

"Eat?" Sudden comprehension flooded the waddy. He went pale with repulsion. "Eat! My God! Oh, my God!"

Miguel glided closer to him, his eyes gleaming strangely, his fingers testing the edge of the knife blade. "What is it, hombre? You sick?"

For a moment the cowboy remained frozen with horror. Then he whirled, scrambled aboard his horse, and spurred away at a dead run.

Miguel looked after him, sheathing his knife slowly. He turned as McClain splashed out of the stream and crossed to him indignantly.

"That was a rotten trick! Fella's scared half outa his wits!"

Miguel looked at him serenely. "I did nothing but tell him the truth."

"The truth?"

"Exactly. I have no money, no gun." He grinned wickedly. "And we have not eaten since last night."

McClain stared at him incredulously for an instant, then he, too, began to grin. "Didn't think the simple truth could spook a man so bad."

"It is the most powerful weapon of Heaven, my friend."

Their eyes met. They burst into laughter.

Four

McClain wakened at dawn the next morning, sharply and without drowsiness; the decision he had reached the night before still uppermost in his mind. He glanced across the dead campfire at Miguel and saw that the priest was still asleep – rolled so tightly in his blankets that only his hat was visible.

The gunfighter sat up. Discarding his sling, he tested his injured arm, straightening it slowly, flexing his fingers. There was stiffness, but very little pain. Only the area around his shoulder and chest remained sore. He opened his shirt and peered awkwardly down at the newly formed scar beneath it. The tissue was still thin and delicate, but it was healthy, without inflammation. Satisfied, McClain rebuttoned the shirt and rose.

"You slept soundly, my friend."

McClain looked up sharply, saw Miguel approaching from the direction of the stream. He was leading the horse and the mule.

The gunfighter scowled, jerked his head toward the priest's rolled blankets. "How come I been campin' with a dummy?"

"I thought it best to keep watch, in case we had more visitors."

"Why didn't y'tell me?"

"You were asleep."

McClain studied him for an instant, then admitted grumpily, "Good idea – watchin'."

Miguel smiled. "So is yours."

"Mine? What're you talkin' about?"

The priest began rubbing down his mule with a handful of marsh grass. "Last night you were deeply thoughtful, like a man with decisions to make." He looked up soberly. "You wish to move on. Right, my friend?"

McClain stared at him, taken aback. Then he replied uncomfortably, "Like you said, we could get more visitors here."

Miguel nodded. "It is wise to make our camp elsewhere." He resumed grooming the mule.

McClain watched him silently, searching his mind for a way to explain the rest of his plans. He was filled suddenly with guilt because he hadn't told the priest about them last night.

At last he blurted harshly, "I'm not movin' camp. I'm hittin' the trail. *Alone.*"

His words didn't seem to surprise Miguel. He said quietly, "You are not yet healed. A few more days of rest would be better."

"There's things I want behind me. This place – that town back there. . . ."

The priest nodded, his face unreadable. "Both animals have been grained. You have only to saddle up."

McClain pulled a piece of sacking from his saddlebags and began rubbing his horse briskly, trying to ignore the guilt building inside of him. After all, he was strong enough to travel. Why should he delay? Why feel such a sense of obligation, of somehow letting his companion down?

"Where will you go, McClain?" Miguel's voice interrupted his thoughts.

The gunfighter shrugged. "Don't know for sure. Maybe California." Without really wanting to, he added, "How about you?"

"My pilgrimage has ended. I must return to my mission. I have been gone from it for many months."

"*You* run a mission?"

Miguel smiled, undisturbed by his astonishment. "I was on my way back there when we met."

The offhand reminder of Miguel's help increased McClain's sense of obligation. He threw the priest a suspicious look, wondering whether the remark was deliberate. Miguel's return glance was open, totally without guile.

"Where is this mission?" asked McClain gruffly.

Miguel replied that it was near a small ranching town called Rileyville. It was an old mission and very poor; so poor that he was the only priest there. He explained wistfully that the people of the town were of other faiths, that they used the mission because it was the only place of worship in the area. Many of the followers came from a tribe of Indians who lived in the nearby hills. They were gentle, childlike people with simple ways and beliefs.

"They are wonderful people," said Miguel fervently, "filled with the joy of living, even though they have very little."

McClain was impressed by the priest's obvious dedication, surprised by this new side to his character. He said soberly, "Sounds like that mission's your whole life."

"It is a fine place for a life. A place of tranquillity and truth." Miguel's face lighted impulsively. "Come and see it, my friend! It isn't far – only a day's ride to the south. You will find peace there, perhaps some answers to your future."

McClain hesitated, then shook his head. "No thanks. I'm not much on missions. I'll just drift till I find out what I'm lookin' for."

Disappointment flooded Miguel's face. "I will miss your company." He glanced at the sun, lifted his saddle quickly to the mule's back. "I must begin my journey while it is early. After dark, the trail to the mission is dangerous for a lone traveler."

McClain stared at him triumphantly. "So that's why y'asked me along! I figured there was more to it than my future!"

Miguel flushed, admitted humbly that there *would* be less danger on the trip for two men, one a well-known gunfighter. He confessed also that the added safety had indeed influenced his thinking, and apologized for his selfishness.

"After all, why should you change your path for me – a stranger you encountered by chance? True, I saved your life, but that is a priest's duty. You owe me nothing for it." He turned his attention to tightening the mule's cinch.

McClain watched him uncomfortably, suspicious of his attitude but unable to dismiss his own sense of guilt. After a moment, he said, "Well, I'm mighty obliged for what y'did, *mighty* obliged. But your mission's directly opposite to the way I'm headin' and . . ." The gunfighter's voice trailed lamely, stemmed by conflicting emotions.

Miguel nodded understandingly. "It is your choice, my friend. You have seen much danger. Why should you face more for me? As I said, you owe me nothing – *absolutely nothing!*"

McClain saddled his horse unhappily, tied his bedroll in place, and mounted. "Well, good luck, *amigo.*"

"Safe journey, my friend. I am glad we met."

His quiet words stirred more guilt in the gunfighter. Touching his hat in a farewell salute, he spurred away hastily.

McClain emerged from the maze of boulders and turned north along the main trail. Reins loose, letting his horse choose its own pace, he sank into brooding thought, still wrestling with his turmoil. His last sight of Miguel, patiently loading his mule, solitary and alone, stood out poignantly in his mind. He remembered that this was a man who had delayed his journey to save McClain's life. A man who had kept the gunfighter's confidences, guarded his weakness, even shared his whiskey with him. The last recollection was too much for *any* Irishman! McClain halted sharply, debated an instant longer, then spun his horse and galloped back toward the camp.

Nearing the camp, the gunfighter saw Miguel preparing to mount up. As he slid his foot into a stirrup, an ominous rattling sounded from the brush beside him. With a startled bray, the mule shied, knocking Miguel down as it raced off. Frozen, Miguel stared at a coiled rattlesnake, its head only inches from his face.

McClain jerked his horse to a stop, called sharply, "Don't move!"

As he spoke, the snake's rattling stopped. In a blur of movement, its head darted for Miguel. In the same instant McClain's gun cleared leather. His bullet caught the reptile in midair. It dropped to the ground with a lifeless thud.

Perspiration beading his forehead, Miguel rose, thanked McClain. The gunfighter nodded, holstering his gun slowly, a gleam of satisfaction in his eyes.

"Glad to even the score some, *amigo.*"

"I, too, am glad," said Miguel fervently. A sudden thought struck him. "But how did you draw so quickly? I thought your fingers were too stiff."

"Arthritis comes an' goes with the weather. When it's like today – hot an' sunny – I can draw as quick as ever. When it's cold or damp, my hands stiffen up." McClain flexed his fingers. He demonstrated by tossing three pebbles into the air, drawing, and shooting them before they fell back to the ground.

"I have never seen such skill!" Miguel's voice rang with awed admiration. "You are a marvel, McClain! And so was the good fortune which brought you back here!"

"It wasn't luck. I just changed my mind – decided to take a look at that mission of yours."

A flicker of craft showed on Miguel's beaming face as he exclaimed, "You are right! It was not luck. It was the will of Heaven!"

Five

McClain rounded up the priest's mule, and the two men rode on together. They followed the main trail for several miles, then Miguel angled southward across the plain toward some hills which huddled against the horizon.

By midafternoon they had crossed the hills and descended to the edge of a broad landscape of mesquite and sand. McClain reined in, scanned the deserted expanse. It stretched, lonely and unbroken, in all directions.

The gunfighter scowled. "Thought your mission was only a day's ride. Looks like we're travelin' over half the country."

"Be patient, my friend. It is only a little farther. We should reach it before sunset."

McClain shifted his squinting scrutiny to Miguel's face. "If it's that close, we oughta be pickin' up some kinda trail."

Miguel nodded serenely. "I am taking a shortcut. We will reach the trail later." He urged his mule forward, angling across the mesquite toward the empty distance.

McClain followed, still scowling dubiously.

At dusk they were still traveling; prairie dog mounds and rabbit holes were the only signs of habitation. Angrily, McClain demanded an explanation and accused Miguel of tricking him.

"You have reason to be angry," said Miguel humbly, "but it is no trick. I have just chosen the wrong shortcut."

"You sayin' we missed the trail?" demanded McClain indignantly.

Miguel nodded unhappily. "I am sorry. But in the morning, when our animals are fresh, we will find it. And then it will take no time to reach the mission."

McClain glared at him suspiciously. "Okay, we'll make camp. But if I don't see walls by noon tomorrow, I'm cuttin' you loose!"

The priest nodded meekly, "I understand." He led the way along a narrow wash to a small spring.

The two men dismounted and unsaddled their tired animals. As McClain staked the pair and fed them from their respective supply sacks of grain, Miguel built a cheery fire. Soon he had coffee and beans heating above the flames.

McClain ate in sour silence, replying shortly to all Miguel's attempts at conversation. When his plate was empty, the gunfighter scoured it with sand and set it aside. Then he rolled up grumpily in his blanket, his back to Miguel and the fire.

For a while he heard the priest scraping dishes and rummaging in his gear, then he fell into a doze. The sharp snap of cards being shuffled and stacked roused him. At first, he thought he was dreaming. When the sounds continued, he turned. Astonished, he saw Miguel hunkered in the firelight, laying out a hand of solitaire with a frayed deck.

McClain elbowed up, asking sourly, "Don't y'ever sleep?"

Miguel shrugged, still intent on the cards. "I am restless tonight." He finished laying out the hand, began to play it.

"How come a priest to be carryin' pasteboards?" asked McClain suspiciously.

Miguel explained serenely that he saw no evil in pieces of pasteboard. The evil was in the hearts of those who used the cards wrongly. To him, they were a means of amusement, nothing more.

"But if my playing disturbs you, my friend, I will stop."

McClain shook his head grumpily. "Play all night if y'want to." He pulled up his blanket and rolled over again.

Miguel threw him a shrewd glance and continued his game, making sure to snap an occasional card sharply as he put it in place. McClain remained motionless for a few minutes, then he turned, sat up, and began to watch the priest.

Miguel was a poor player, and seemingly an inexperienced one. With growing impatience, McClain pointed out his mistakes to him. At last the priest shrugged, admitted wryly that solitaire was not his game.

"I am better at the one they play in saloons."

"Poker?" asked McClain incredulously.

Miguel nodded. "Yes, that is the name. Do you know it?"

McClain studied him narrowly. "I played a little."

Miguel's face lighted eagerly. "Shall we play now? It will pass the time."

"What stakes?"

Miguel seemed shocked. "A priest does not wager, my friend! I play only for amusement."

"They don't play for amusement in saloons."

Miguel met his doubting eyes blandly. "I do not play in saloons. I only watch. That is how I learned the game."

McClain snorted. "That's no way t'learn! You gotta sit in on every game you can."

"So that is the way!" The priest looked impressed. "I would like to learn more. Perhaps you will teach me."

Still suspicious, McClain started to refuse,

then decided to test him. "Deal," he ordered.

Clumsily, Miguel dealt a hand of draw. McClain found himself holding a pair of aces. He won easily when the priest overlooked a small straight and folded without calling. He revealed his mistake wryly, suggested they play again.

Convinced that he had a sucker, McClain agreed, but insisted that the game held no interest for him without wagers. Miguel hesitated, then agreed reluctantly to risk a few pesos. During the next four hands, he lost them quickly and consistently, misjudged his cards, and revealed his ignorance further by asking whether three of a kind was higher than two pair. After each hand, McClain raked in the pesos and gave him good-humored pointers. The gunfighter had begun to enjoy himself immensely.

Soon Miguel's small pile of coins was stacked before McClain. Pleased, the gunfighter started to pocket his winnings.

"Sorry y'didn't come out better, *amigo,* but you got a lot t'learn about this game."

Miguel agreed meekly and suggested that they play some more so he could practice the things McClain had taught him.

"What're you gonna use for money?" asked the gunfighter.

"I have a few more pesos in my saddlebags."

"Okay," said McClain smugly, "least I can do is give you a chance t'get even."

Miguel produced a handful of bills and coins from his gear and laid the money on the ground in front of him. "Deal, my friend," said the priest eagerly.

McClain shuffled deftly, thinking that this trip to the mission wasn't such a bad idea after all. Half an hour later he'd begun to change his mind. Miguel's luck had improved, and so had his card sense. He'd won three hands in a row, calling McClain's bluff on two of them and outbluffing the gunfighter on the third. Half McClain's winnings were already gone.

"Your playin' sure improved fast," remarked the gunfighter sourly.

"That is due to your fine teaching, my friend." Miguel smiled at him appreciatively, pushed ten dollars into the pot, and raised another ten.

McClain matched the raise and laid down a jack-high straight. Humbly, declaring it was beginner's luck, Miguel spread out his cards, revealing a flush.

Sure that the priest's winning streak was a fluke, McClain upped the size of his bets and the shrewdness of his betting. Soon he had lost everything, including his horse and saddle.

Miguel was incredulous at his sudden success. He insisted contritely that they must play a hand of "showdown" so McClain would have a chance to recoup his losses.

"What am I gonna bet? My skin?" asked the gunfighter angrily.

For an instant, Miguel hesitated, crestfallen. Then his face brightened. "Your skin. *Of course!* That is a fine idea!"

"What d'you mean a fine idea?"

Miguel grinned. "It is very simple, my friend. You will wager two weeks of your services at my mission against the pot."

"What's a priest need with a gunfighter?" asked McClain suspiciously.

Miguel explained that the mission was isolated. Occasionally there were intruders. He could use some protection until the Indians learned he was back and came in from the hills.

"Of course, if you do not like the terms . . ." He gave McClain a concerned look. "But by what other means can you try to change your luck, my friend?"

McClain glared at him, getting the point. "Deal!" he ordered harshly.

Happily, Miguel obeyed. A ten to McClain, a five for himself . . . a king to McClain, a jack for himself. McClain's third card was another king. The priest's was a seven.

"Lady Luck's changin'!" gloated the gunfighter.

Miguel nodded, pleased. "As I hoped, my friend. As I hoped!"

He continued dealing, dropping each card carefully, face up. McClain got another ten, giving him two pair with only one more card to go. The gunfighter whooped triumphantly as Miguel got another seven. "Not good enough!"

Miguel shrugged good-naturedly and dealt McClain his last card. It was a seven.

The gunfighter's face split in a grin. "Looks like my game!"

Miguel hesitated, then slowly turned up *his* last card. McClain stared at it strickenly. It was a third seven! *The case seven!*

"I am sorry, McClain – truly sorry."

McClain straightened, realizing he'd been had. His face went dark with rage and he jerked out his gun.

"You no good, bottom-dealin' . . . ! Y'sharked me in!"

"You accuse a *priest* of cheating?"

"I'm not even sure you *are* a priest!" McClain shoved the gun against Miguel's chest. "But I'm gonna make sure, 'cause I'd *kill* anybody else who cheated me at poker!"

Miguel shook his head sadly. "To accuse a priest of cheating! You have no faith, my friend."

Six

McClain and the priest rode through the bright morning sun for two hours before they cut the trail to the mission. It was little more than a deer path, and it wound upward through gentle hills toward a high plateau. Trees began to appear among the boulders, and the undergrowth grew more lush. The smells were clean and good, and the birds scolded melodiously as the two men rode past.

Usually McClain enjoyed such country, but today his mind was filled with a strange uneasiness, his nerves tight from the sharp instinct which always warned him when someone was following him. He couldn't explain the feeling, but he'd had it all his life. It had saved him from death many times. Today it was strong and insistent, making him turn frequently in his saddle to scan the path behind them.

Miguel noticed his preoccupation and halted, asking curiously, "What is it, McClain? What is bothering you?"

"There's somebody on our back trail," said

the gunfighter tightly, “my gut’s been warnin’ me ever since we broke camp.”

“How can you be sure?”

“I can feel it. I always can.” As McClain spoke, his horse cupped its ears back, listening to something behind them which was inaudible to the men. The gunfighter recognized the signal instantly. “See his ears? He knows it, too.”

Miguel nodded sober agreement. “Perhaps it is only another traveler. Let us wait in the brush and see.”

They pushed through the brush to a stand of trees and concealed themselves, dismounting and waiting tensely, each ready to cover his mount’s nostrils if it started to whicker.

Soon Hal Peters rode slowly into view, his eyes searching the path. Startled, McClain and Miguel recognized him. They watched uneasily as he halted near where they’d left the trail, scrutinized the ground for their tracks. He saw nothing. The brush had sprung into place behind them, leaving no trace of their passing, and the profusion of deer prints on the path made those of their mounts indistinguishable. At last, Peters rode on, assuming the two men were still ahead of him.

McClain looked after him, angry frustration in his eyes. “Damn kid! I figured he might track me. Won’t be satisfied till one of us is dead."

"He is evil," agreed Miguel, "a true killer." He frowned bewilderedly. "But how did he discover you were alive? That is what puzzles me."

McClain gave him a wry look. "Probably don't believe in *cannibals* any more than *I* would. Went to the stream to take a look for himself and picked up our trail from there."

"We should have covered our tracks more carefully, my friend."

McClain shook his head in grim negation. "Wouldn't have helped. Some things y'can't hide – or run from, either. Peters is one of 'em." He flexed his fingers experimentally. The sun had warmed them. They felt fine. He said, "It's a good day t'face him. Might as well get it over with."

He turned to mount his horse, but Miguel caught his arm urgently. "You said you had given up killing!"

"Not if I have to die t'do it," said McClain dryly. He started to mount, but Miguel's grip on his arm tightened.

"Have you forgotten our wager, McClain?"

"What the hell are you gettin' at?"

Miguel's blue eyes met his sternly. "You lost your skin to me last night, my friend. You cannot risk it until you have repaid your gambling debt."

McClain glared at him. "I'll pay it when I'm done with Peters."

"That is not fair. Suppose you are killed?"

The gunfighter was outraged. "That all you can think of? What I owe you?"

"Such a thing is a debt of honor, is it not?" insisted Miguel.

Their eyes held in stubborn conflict, McClain angrily aware that the priest had snared him with his own unbreakable code. No man of his breed left a gambling debt unpaid.

The gunfighter acknowledged his defeat explosively. "Why, you no-good, sneaky, sidewindin' . . . ! You call yourself a *priest?*"

Miguel smiled. "Heaven works in strange ways, my friend." He mounted his mule. "There is a canyon nearby which leads to another trail. We will travel that way to the mission. Then we will not meet Peters."

He urged the mule through dense brush and entered a narrow, rocky defile. McClain followed reluctantly, still glowering.

The canyon ascended steeply, cutting through rising hills to end abruptly on a ridge overlooking a high, rolling mountain valley. As the two men stopped to let their animals breathe a moment, McClain saw that the valley was lush and green, protected on three sides by the hills. A wagon road followed the base of the hills to the mouth of the valley, which merged with a distant, undulating plain.

Miguel pointed toward the plain. "My mission lies just beyond the hills. The road passes close to it."

"Longest day's ride I ever took," remarked McClain sourly.

They descended to the wagon road, followed it at a steady jog until, rounding a turn, they found their path barred by an overturned, scorched Conestoga wagon. They reined in sharply, staring in shock at the disaster.

The wagon was bristling with arrows, its canvas top burned, its sides battered so badly that the words "Lathrop Mine" were barely readable. Its driver and two guards lay beside the vehicle, dead, their bodies pinned to the ground with feathered spears. There was no sign of their weapons or of the wagon's cargo.

The two men dismounted to examine the wreckage more closely. It was stripped clean of all equipment, and the surrounding hoofprints indicated that even its team of workhorses had been appropriated by the attackers.

McClain poked curiously at a splintered plank. "Wonder what she was carryin'."

Miguel was studying the feathered spears with a heartbroken expression. "Bullion," he said, "gold bullion."

McClain looked at him, startled by the anguish in his voice, puzzled by the whole situation. "Never heard of Indians attackin' for gold before. Thought you said the tribes around here were peaceful."

"Sometimes peace must be defended, my friend." Miguel knelt sadly beside the fallen men, his crucifix in his hand. For a long moment his lips moved in silent prayer. Then he passed his open hands above the bodies, murmuring a final benediction, and rose. His attitude changed abruptly from reverence to urgency. "Come, McClain," he said, "we must hurry."

He mounted his mule, guided it around the wreckage, and urged it along the road beyond at a rolling lope. McClain galloped after him, indignation mixed with his bewilderment. He brought his horse even with the mule.

"Hey, where you goin'? Those men back there need buryin'!"

Miguel turned a coldly determined face to him. "There is no time," he answered harshly. "Something worse than death has happened here."

As he spoke, they heard loud male voices ahead. They mingled with the thud of picks and shovels and the rattling of chains. The sounds seemed to fill Miguel with alarm. Ordering McClain curtly to follow him, the priest led the way into the brush. Behind a stand of trees, they tied their animals and crawled quietly to the top of a boulder-strewn rise.

Below them, in the side of a hill, was a small mine. A group of staggering, emaciated Indians, their ankles chained, were working the mine. Two husky, tough-faced guards, armed with rifles and heavy whips, directed the work with shouts and blows. The two men watched in stunned horror.

"Madre de Dios! They are enslaved!" Miguel rose to his feet, staring down at the scene, trancelike, his horror increasing as the pitiable condition of the Indians became more apparent.

"Get down!" hissed McClain. "Get down!"

Miguel ignored his warning, moved further into the open, his eyes wide and tortured. "My people, my poor, ravaged people!"

Suddenly one of the Indians glanced up and saw him. Terror convulsed the Indian's features. He dropped the heavy sack he was carrying and pointed shakily toward Miguel, shrieking, *"Padre Diablo! Padre Diablo!"*

Startled, the other Indians looked toward the priest. Fear mingled with the recognition on their faces. Echoing their companion's shrieks, they tried to flee, dragging their chains, stumbling, falling.

Miguel remained frozen, watching, deaf to

McClain's frantic warnings to get out of sight. As the guards converged on the Indians, driving them back toward the mine, shouting and lashing them unmercifully, McClain jerked the priest back to concealment among the boulders.

"Let's make tracks!" ordered the gunman harshly.

Miguel gave him a blank look. Cursing, McClain gripped the priest's arm, forced him down the rise to his mule.

"Ride!" he ordered. "Ride!" He slapped the mule's rump sharply with the flat of his hand.

As the animal lurched into a gallop, Miguel snapped back to reality. Guiding the mule on a zigzag course through brush and trees, McClain's horse pounding behind them, the priest led the way across the valley toward the plain beyond it.

When the bedlam at the mine could no longer be heard, Miguel pulled his lathered mule to a walk. McClain slowed his horse to the same pace, wiped dust and sweat from his eyes with his neckerchief, then gave Miguel a narrowed, measuring glance.

"Mind tellin' me what that ruckus back there was all about?" asked the gunman caustically.

Miguel looked up sadly, pulling himself from brooding thought. "I do not know, Mc-

Clain. I cannot even tell you why the Indians were so afraid of me."

McClain snorted skeptically. "I suppose y'don't know why they called you a devil, either."

"I can explain nothing," insisted Miguel. "I only know that they are my people – members of the tribe which I serve. I know each of their faces, each of their hearts. I have nursed them during illness, guided them spiritually. . . ." He paused, then added raggedly, "I am their priest, like a father to them."

McClain remained skeptical. "Sure," he said pointedly, *"Father Devil."*

Seven

Miguel led the way out of the valley and across the deserted plain beyond at a steady jog, his face set into lines of anxiety. Soon he and McClain sighted the mission. It crouched on the arid land, isolated and lonely, its color so similar to the surrounding sand that from a distance it was hardly discernible.

As the two men rode closer, McClain saw that it was a small place, consisting only of the main chapel and a modest wing, but its thick adobe walls and the matching wall which enclosed its courtyard were constructed to withstand the onslaughts of time and weather. A slim tower sprang upward from its chapel roof, displaying an ancient iron bell which hung from its covered belfry. As the gunfighter looked, a gust of wind raged briefly across the plain. It struck the bell, stirring it slightly. A deep, resounding knell echoed over the land, rending the silence with somber authority, and carrying for miles.

At the sound, Miguel reined in sharply, the

anxiety on his face increasing.

"What's the matter?" asked McClain irritably. The bell had set his ears ringing uncomfortably.

"The bell! It should not be tolling!"

"That's a fact! It's enough t'bust a man's eardrums!"

Miguel nodded absently, his concerned gaze still on the distant mission. "It was fashioned by the finest artisans. Its sound carries for almost ten miles." He turned his worried eyes to McClain. "But the wind should not stir it. Its restraints must be broken."

His manner puzzled McClain. "Maybe so. What about it?"

"They are heavy chains. They would not break accidentally."

"You thinkin' there's been trouble at the mission?"

"Yes." Digging his heels into the mule's flanks, Miguel set off at a wild gallop which didn't slow until the two men reached the courtyard gate.

As their mounts slid to a halt, they saw that the gate was flung wide, the yard choked with weeds. The chapel door was ajar – hanging on broken hinges and scarred by bullet holes.

Miguel sat motionless and stricken for a moment. Then he dismounted and entered the courtyard slowly; his heartbroken glance taking in the devastation with disbelief.

"The tribe must have sought refuge here and tolled the bell for help which never came." Anguished self-reproach twisted the priest's face.

McClain remained mounted, eyes raking the scene, suspicious of its strange emptiness. He could find no trace of movement or ambush, and at last he stepped to the ground, moved across the courtyard cautiously – still alert for trouble. Suddenly he noticed a lone grave in a corner of the inner wall. He crossed to read the wooden marker at its head. The epitaph was brief: *"Here lies Father Miguel."*

"Madre de Dios!" Miguel's horrified voice whirled the gunfighter around. The priest stood at his elbow, staring at the grave.

Fury surged through McClain like bitter gall. "So that's your game! The priest's dead an' you're takin' his place! You brought me here for a lie!"

Miguel stared at him, tortured. "No, McClain, you are wrong! This grave is the lie!"

McClain's gun cleared leather and rammed into Miguel's abdomen. "Quit double-talkin'! I want the truth!"

"You saw it at the mine. A people are enslaved!" Miguel ignored the gun, met his accusing eyes steadily.

McClain's fury increased. "What's that got

to do with me, *priest?*"

"What did the Indian at the saloon have to do with you?"

"That was different. He was a soldier."

"So are the Indians here – warriors and humans. If one matters to you, all must."

The words had no effect on McClain. His gun dug deeper into Miguel's stomach. "Quit coyotin' around and tell me who you are!"

"I swear on this grave that I am Father Miguel, the priest of this mission."

The urgency in his voice and face struck McClain. His rage cooled, and the sense of disappointed betrayal which had spawned it lessened. He lowered his gun, gestured toward the grave. "If you're the priest, who's that?"

Miguel shook his head sadly. "I have been gone six months. I only know that the grave was not here when I left."

"I figure you've got more to tell than that."

"Yes, much more. I only beg you to believe me."

Suspicion remained strong on McClain's face. "Go on," he ordered coldly, still standing with his gun in hand.

Eight

Miguel sank down on a rough wooden bench which stood near the grave and began to speak, his face filled with bitterness and self-reproach.

"Six months ago, the Indians here were prosperous and happy. Their camp was in the hills, near the mine which you saw. To them it is a sacred cave – the property of their tribe for many centuries." Miguel paused, fighting to control his emotions for an instant, then continued. "There was loose gold in the cave. 'Yellow rocks,' the Indians called it. Its value meant nothing to them, but they sometimes made it into trinkets and brought them to the mission as altar offerings."

"What kinda trinkets?" asked McClain.

"Necklaces, bracelets, small statues of the saints. They are very clever people, and very devout."

"Mighty handsome offerings. What did y'do with 'em? Sell 'em?"

Miguel looked at him sadly. "How little you trust me, my friend."

"I don't trust a coyote in a chicken house, either," answered McClain.

"I can understand your doubts," said Miguel humbly, "but I am not a thief, McClain. The offerings belong to the mission. They were meant to be used only in its service."

"So where are they?"

"They were in a secret place beneath the altar. Stored for safekeeping."

"What d'you mean *were?*" McClain demanded sharply.

Miguel slumped on the bench. "I will come to that, McClain." He went on with his story emotionally. "The Indians knew that white men valued their 'yellow rocks.' They asked me never to reveal how I got the altar offerings. I swore a sacred vow with their tribal chief not to do so." Memories darkened his eyes. "I meant to keep the vow, but somehow Lathrop and his men learned of the trinkets."

"Lathrop? That was the name on the bullion wagon!"

Miguel nodded. "He is a ruthless man. He and his gang are feared by everyone. Even the town of Rileyville dares not stand against Lathrop's men."

"I take it they headquarter in these parts."

"Yes. Lathrop poses as a rancher. In reality, he is a thief and a murderer." Hatred filled Miguel's face for an instant. Then he went on miserably, "They came here one night. Lathrop and five others. They forced their way into the chapel and demanded to know where the gold was. I tried to deny any knowledge of it, but they beat me until I told them everything . . . even the location of the tribal cave." Miguel buried his face in his hands, agonized.

Voice breaking, he told how the outlaws tore away the altar cloth and took the offerings from their hiding place. Then, leaving him for dead, they headed for the Indian camp. Somehow he dragged himself to his mule and went to the nearby town of Rileyville for help.

"But the people were too afraid of Lathrop. They would not help me, McClain. They wanted to drive me away. All of them except one . . . a young woman. Brave and pure as a saint! She is called Annie Johnson. She insisted on hiding me, nursing me until I was strong enough to travel. She begged for me! Begged until the others agreed to let me stay. But only if I promised to leave as soon as possible and never return." Shame flooded Miguel's face. "To save my miserable life, I gave them my word. A week later I left. I cannot explain about the grave or tell you why I am called 'devil.' I only know that I spent six months searching for a way to bring Lathrop to justice. You were the answer I prayed for, McClain."

McClain stared at him, a mixture of sympathy and bewilderment on his face. "You're still talkin' puzzles," he said.

"No! It is very clear! With a famous gunfighter to lead them, the people here will take courage. They will unite and drive Lathrop out. Then the Indians will be free again . . . and so will I." His pleading eyes met the gunfighter's urgently.

McClain hesitated uncomfortably, then asked, "Ain't there some kinda law around here? A marshal or somebody?"

"There have been two sheriffs. Lathrop's men made sure they did not stay long."

"Why should I take on a fight that's not mine?"

"You fought against slavery before."

"That's how I learned t'mind my own business. And I don't plan t'change that learnin'." McClain holstered his gun and scowled stubbornly at the priest. "So you better figure a different way for me t'pay off my bet."

Miguel rose with a sigh. "I know I tricked you into coming here, my friend. But the need is desperate. I hoped you would understand that." He fixed McClain with a solemn stare. "Just as *I* understood *your* need when I found you at the stream."

His meaning was sharply clear. It cut at the gunfighter like a knife, sending a thrust of guilt through him. He scowled and reminded Miguel that he wasn't a top gunfighter anymore – except on sunny days.

"And since a lotta days ain't sunny, I'm liable t'end up in a quick grave. Now why should I risk that for a poker-cheatin' snake like you?"

His words shook Miguel with sudden, face-crumbling shame. "You are right. There is no reason, my friend. I am a coward who deserves nothing from any man."

McClain accepted his admission uneasily. "Well, at least you're man enough t'own up to it."

"I admit also that I have tricked you enough. Go! I release you from your bargain. Take your property and go!" Miguel turned forlornly toward the chapel.

McClain watched him, taken aback by his sudden change of attitude. "Where *you* goin'?"

The priest continued toward the chapel door. "To pray," he answered.

McClain shook his head bewilderedly, then started toward his horse. A sudden thought made him pause and call out. "What happens if Lathrop finds out you're alive?"

"He'll hang me." Miguel disappeared into the chapel.

McClain glared after him for a moment, angry at his conflicting emotions. Then, with a distracted curse, he mounted his horse and rode off in the direction of Rileyville.

From the shadows beyond the ravaged chapel door, Miguel watched him speculatively, the humble dejection of a few minutes earlier completely gone from his manner.

Nine

The chained Indians huddled together, shaking their heads and shrieking the name *"Padre Diablo,"* refusing to enter the mine despite curses and blows from their two guards.

At last the guards hauled an elderly Indian from the group and shoved a pistol against his forehead. Angrily, they announced that unless work in the mine resumed, the man would be shot.

As the prisoners fell silent, exchanging uneasy glances, the old Indian squared his shoulders and shouted, "Do not hear them! The cave is taboo now! *Padre Diablo* has put evil spirits there!"

The guard with the pistol increased its pressure against the old man's temple. "Shut up!" he yelled. He eyed the other tribesmen threateningly. "This fleabag is your chief's father. Do you work or does he die?"

The Indians hesitated, whispered among themselves. Then a young warrior fixed the guards with a savage glare. "We cannot let these dogs shed the old one's blood," he cried. "We will work."

Cursing, the second guard brought his whip down across the young warrior's shoulders as his companion shoved the old Indian back into line. Trembling and reluctant, the prisoners filed into the cave, the guards prodding them brutally.

As work resumed, Bart Lathrop, a heavyset, shrewd-eyed man of about forty, rode to a halt near the cave entrance. He sat watching the activity, holding his restless, highly bred mount in check expertly. A coldly magnetic figure, he was expensively dressed, his saddle richly tooled and studded with silver. Two stony-faced, thin-lipped gunmen rode with him.

Lathrop was a canny, totally amoral leader of men who stopped at nothing to get and keep what he wanted. He was known for his fancy clothes, unscrupulous methods, and thirst for power. His followers consisted of twenty hard-cases, all as cold-blooded and dangerous as their leader.

The gang's domain extended from the hills to the plain and the ranching town of Rileyville, which they dominated through terror and treachery. Until Lathrop discovered the existence of the Indian mine, their activities were limited to robberies and rustling. Now the gang was rapidly accumulating a wealth of gold, and Lathrop congratulated himself frequently on the luck which had brought a certain golden trinket to his attention.

Lathrop's sharp-eyed gaze quickly noted the Indians' uneasiness. "What's botherin' 'em?" he asked the guards. "They're actin' funny."

One of the guards replied diffidently. "They're scared, Mr. Lathrop. Claim they saw that dead priest from the mission standin' on the hill."

Lathrop frowned. "Father Miguel?"

"That's right. Only now they're callin' him *'Padre Diablo.'* They swear he's hooked up with the devil 'cause he broke some kinda promise while he was alive. They think he's come back to turn evil spirits loose on 'em."

Lathrop scanned the surrounding hills narrowly. "You boys see anything in the hills?"

"Nothin' at all," replied the guard.

Lathrop's face cleared. "Then forget it. Damn savages are probably tryin' to get out of workin'. Give the next one that sees a devil twenty lashes. That'll take the spook out of 'em."

Lathrop spun his horse and galloped away toward town. The two gunmen followed him.

Except for periodic, brawling visits from Lathrop's men, Rileyville was a small, serene town. Its main street was lined with neatly painted stores, one selling dry goods, one feed and grain, and one grocery supplies. There was a Chinese laundry, a livery stable, a blacksmith, a boardinghouse, and at the far end of the street, the town's only saloon. All the establishments owed their prosperity to the success of the many surrounding ranches. The town itself existed because of them and because of their owners' need for some semblance of civilization amid the vast emptiness which surrounded them. It was a place where they could herd together and forget for a while that they were intruders in this lonely, savage land.

McClain's horse was tied in front of the saloon between two others. Except for the animals and several men lounging in front of the livery stable, the street was deserted.

Inside the honkytonk, unimaginatively named "Cattlemen's Saloon," McClain was the only customer at the bar. Three middle-aged men, all in city clothes, sat at a nearby table drinking beer and eyeing the gunfighter uneasily. They were the mayor, Horace Spencer, the boardinghouse owner, Jake Gulden, and Emmet Fowler, the chairman of the town council. The husky bartender and an attractive, bosomy saloon hostess were the only others present. They, too, eyed McClain with sober curiosity.

The gunfighter was aware of their interest and of the undercurrents of uneasiness which accompanied it. He had sensed the tension as soon as he entered, and wondered resentfully what it meant.

As he drained his whiskey glass, his mind still broodingly occupied with Miguel, the mayor called out cheerfully, "Next drink's on us, stranger."

McClain had expected some such invitation. He frowned, preferring to be left alone, then turned, his face carefully unreadable. "Much obliged. Any special reason?"

The three men smiled with exaggerated heartiness. "Customary town welcome, that's all," replied Mayor Spencer. He rose, introduced himself and his companions, and asked McClain's name. The gunfighter supplied it reluctantly, felt relieved when the men seemed not to recognize it.

"What brings you to Rileyville?" asked Chairman Fowler as the bartender refilled McClain's glass.

McClain knew instantly that this was the key question. "Just seein' the country. Be pushin' on when my horse's rested."

The relief on their faces puzzled him. Then he dismissed it and raised his glass to them. "Well, here's to you, gents." He tossed the whiskey down neatly and turned back to the bar, his attitude discouraging further conversation.

Undisturbed by his dismissal, the three townsmen exchanged satisfied glances and resumed talking, showing no further curiosity about him. As the gunfighter continued to drink, the hostess approached him.

"Want some company, stranger?" Her voice was soft and sweet, in striking contrast to her painted face and garish costume.

The sweetness brought McClain a sudden image of Em, and turned his negative head shake into a curt "Why not?"

The girl leaned against the bar, tilted her head so she could see his eyes better, and said with an inviting smile, "I'm Annie Johnson."

For an instant McClain was taken aback. Then he burst into sardonic laughter. "Annie Johnson, huh? I should've figured!"

"What's so funny?" asked the hostess defensively.

"An hombre named Miguel," chuckled McClain, "calls himself *Father* Miguel."

Annie stiffened nervously. "Who? Dunno what you're talkin' about."

McClain met her eyes levelly. "Funny – he knows you."

The girl's nervousness increased. "Mission used to have a priest by that name . . ."

"I'm not sure he's a priest, but I know he's a prime liar."

"Must be another fella. The priest who was here – he's dead."

"Rides a big, scraggly old mule." McClain watched her reaction narrowly, saw the flash of recognition which she tried to hide.

She hesitated uneasily, then leaned closer and glanced around to make sure nobody was listening. "This fella – you got a score against him?"

"Owe him a gamblin' debt."

Relief showed in her eyes. She ran a hand caressingly up his arm, spoke with soft, husky invitation. "Let's talk in my room, okay?"

Her manner intrigued McClain. "What's the price?"

She raised her voice so everyone could overhear. "Four bucks, stranger."

"Fair enough." McClain picked up his whiskey bottle. "Lead on, saintly lady." He gave her a mocking bow and followed as she led the way quickly toward a rear stairway.

Ten

Lathrop and the two gunmen who had accompanied him from the mine strode noisily through the batwings and headed for a table. As they sat down, Lathrop spotted Annie and McClain ascending the stairs.

He frowned, called sharply, "Hey, Annie! Where you goin'? Come on down here!"

The hostess froze, gave McClain a scared look. "We'll talk later," she whispered.

She started down, but the gunfighter put a firm hand on her arm. His gaze met Lathrop's coolly. "She's busy, friend." He resumed climbing the stairs, taking Annie with him.

Lathrop's face blackened with fury. He rose, his companions doing the same. "I want her down here. Pronto!"

McClain turned. "No can do. You'll have t'wait."

Lathrop gestured sharply to his men. They started forward, then one of them suddenly recognized McClain. He halted abruptly and turned back to Lathrop. "Boss, that's Glint

McClain!" he whispered.

The outlaw leader gave him a startled look. "You sure?"

The man nodded. "We used t'hang out in the same town. Played poker with him."

Lathrop looked toward the gunfighter. McClain had descended to the bottom of the stairs. He was waiting, eyes narrowed and wary. He looked as dangerous as a crouched cougar.

Lathrop's face smoothed as if wiped with a damp towel. "Looks like there's been a little mistake." He nodded toward the man beside him. "Rafe here says you're a buddy of his – Glint McClain."

Rafe said hastily, "Mesa City, Glint. Recollect?"

McClain's militant scrutiny changed to recognition. "Rafe Cluny, right?" His tone was friendly but not enthusiastic.

"Right! Been a long time!"

McClain nodded agreement, then looked at Lathrop. "The lady's *still* busy," he said pointedly.

Lathrop smiled good-naturedly. "That bein' the case, I'll wait my turn."

"Good."

"By the way, I'm Bart Lathrop – Rafe's boss." The tension in the room eased as Lathrop extended his hand and McClain took it.

Their handshake was hard and competitive,

each man taking the other's measure. Lathrop was the first to loosen his grip. His eyes glittered dangerously at the defeat, but his manner remained friendly.

"Heard a lot about you, McClain. What brings you to Rileyville?"

"Just driftin'."

"Open for a job? My outfit could use a top gun."

McClain's face remained carefully unreadable. "What would I be gunnin' for?"

"I've got a little gold mine up in the hills. Need protection for my bullion wagons – among other things."

McClain considered thoughtfully. "Like I said, I'm just driftin' through. But I could pause awhile if the job pays enough."

"Pays just about whatever you want. Long as you do whatever *I* want."

Their eyes met levelly for a moment, then McClain said, "I'll think on it. Let you know." He turned abruptly and ascended the stairs to the waiting girl. Sliding an arm around her, he drew her through the corridor archway and out of sight.

Lathrop looked after them narrowly, the geniality gone from his face. "McClain's mighty high-handed."

Rafe nodded. "Always was, boss. Calls his own tune."

"He as fast with a gun as I heard?"

"Draws quicker than a strikin' rattler. I know. I seen him gun one down."

"He better be that good. I don't like t'be kept waitin'." Giving Rafe an ominous glare, Lathrop sat down at the table. Hurriedly, the bartender brought them a bottle and some glasses.

Annie led McClain to a small, sparsely furnished room. She closed the door behind them and bolted it carefully. McClain tossed his hat at a bedpost, sat down wearily beside a three-legged table with some glasses on it. He turned up two of the glasses and began to fill them as Annie crossed to him, unbuttoning her dress.

"How do you want your lovin'?" There were nervous undercurrents in her businesslike tone.

"First we talk."

Annie evaded his probing glance. "Father Miguel's not a popular subject around here."

"You act like he's a *dangerous* subject."

"It's best t'let the dead be."

The gunfighter studied her narrowly. "You sayin' the priest's *really* dead?"

The question seemed to increase Annie's uneasiness. She dropped into the chair opposite McClain and downed the whiskey he'd poured for her hastily.

"Sure the priest's dead. He's buried at the mission."

McClain gave her a long, steady look. "Now, that's what I've gotta decide. *Is* he buried or is he a double-dealin' varmint pretendin' t'be somethin' he's not."

Annie's reaction was totally unexpected. Her nervousness changed to sudden, hot anger. "Double-dealin' varmint? That's a lie! Maybe he slipped a little as a priest, but he was the finest man I ever knew."

"Hard t'believe that. Maybe you knew him better than I do."

Annie glared at him. "I knew him real well! And for a long time!"

McClain refilled her glass. He said, "The Miguel I know saved my life, then cheated me. I'd like t'hear about the one *you* knew."

"He'd never cheat anybody! Never!" Annie drained her glass again and stared into space broodingly as McClain filled it.

The gunfighter waited, seeing that the whiskey was mellowing her, releasing memories that she needed to share. After a moment, her eyes misted and she continued sadly.

"He ran into some trouble – real bad trouble. This whole town was part of it, and so was I."

McClain's face was carefully unreadable.

"What kinda trouble?" he probed quietly.

Engrossed in the past now, Annie told the gunfighter the full story of the mission tragedy. Her face soft and wistful, she described Father Miguel as a priest devoted to his duties; one who judged nobody and even allowed *her*, a saloon girl, to attend Sunday services. The town thoroughly disapproved of the priest and his unorthodox viewpoint, even misunderstood his friendship with her.

"Misunderstood? How do you mean?" asked McClain.

Annie ignored the question for a moment, lapsed more deeply into brooding remembrances. "They twisted everything about him. Made it ugly. They thought he was like they are – deceitful and mean. They even thought he did too much for the Indians, that they were heathens and didn't deserve much attention."

McClain broke into her reverie carefully. "What about you and him – your friendship?"

Annie gave him a bitter look. "I went to the mission every day to help him teach the Indian children. It meant a lot – made me feel useful for the first time in my life. But that's all there was to it! There was nothing else! No matter *what* this damn town thinks!"

"Just what does it think?"

Annie pulled up her sleeve, showed him a

gold arm band with Indian symbols on it. "They think he gave me this 'cause we were lovers."

McClain stared at the arm band, realized with a stab of dismay that it was one of the altar offerings Miguel had mentioned to him. Doubts about the priest's sincerity flooded him again.

"Why *did* he give it to you?" he demanded harshly.

Shame filled Annie's face. " 'Cause I wanted it so bad. I knew it was an offering, but I never had any real jewelry before. And it was so beautiful!" Her voice broke for a moment. Then she went on raggedly, "I knew he wanted me to have it. But he said it wasn't his to give. He even prayed about it. That's when he let me have it. He said Heaven had made him see that it would be a gift of thanks from the mission – for my help with the Indian kids."

McClain was moved by her obvious sincerity. "Sounds like somethin' he'd say."

"I only wore it under my dress . . . like now. Never showed it to anybody. Never planned to." Her eyes glazed with heartbreak. "But one night Lathrop came here. I was takin' a bath. I didn't expect him. He just kicked open the door and busted in." She was close to tears. She fought them back. "He knew right away the arm band was real. He made me tell him where I got it. Then he took his men and rode out to the mission." She began to tremble. McClain poured her another drink and she gulped it hastily. "They beat Father Miguel till he was half dead, made him tell them where the Indians got their gold. Then they attacked the tribe – took their land and most of their people."

"So now Lathrop's in the gold-mining business."

Annie nodded bitterly. "Father Miguel tried to stop him. He rode into town that night and stood in the middle of the street and yelled till everybody came out. I'll never forget how he looked, all covered with blood, so weak he could hardly keep from falling. He told everything that happened, put all the blame on himself, said he was weak and scared. He begged the town t'help him save the Indians. Said he could lead them on a shortcut so they could head Lathrop off." Annie's features twisted contemptuously. "They listened and stared till he fell down in the dirt. But they never lifted a finger against Lathrop." Annie finished speaking and slumped back in her chair. "You still think he's a cheat?"

McClain remained silent, sorting out his conflicting thoughts and emotions. Annie had shown him an entirely new side of Miguel, described a noble, heroic figure who deserved the distinction of priesthood. McClain was impressed and moved, but he wondered which image was the true Miguel – Annie's or his own. Or was the priest a combination of the two?

Annie's voice brought him out of his reverie. "There never was anybody like him. I guess there never will be."

McClain considered her thoughtfully for a moment, then asked, "What about the grave?"

The girl straightened warily, fighting against the effects of the whiskey she'd drunk. "I told you. It's his."

"If it is, I been travelin' with a corpse."

Shock brought Annie to her feet. "Travelin'! What . . . what're you sayin'?"

"Miguel's back. He's at the mission. Rode in with me this mornin'." McClain's hand darted to clutch her arm with relentless fingers. He jerked her down to face him. "Now quit coverin'! Who's in that grave?"

"You're hurtin' me!"

"Who's in it?"

"They rigged it. The mayor and his bunch. To keep Lathrop from findin' out somebody helped Miguel."

"You sayin' it's empty?"

Annie nodded whitely. "They wanted t'leave him in the street, but I promised to keep him out of sight. So they let me nurse him for a week – just long enough so he could stay on his mule. Then they made me send him on." Bitterness harshened her voice. "The lousy cowards told Lathrop they found his body an' buried it."

McClain released her arm. "Lathrop's in for a little surprise. Padre's come back t'haunt him into freein' the Indians."

Annie clutched his shirt, her face contorted with fear. "He can't stay! Lathrop'll kill him, and the town'll help!" Her voice rose hysterically. "You gotta make him leave! He won't have a chance!"

McClain nodded tightly, rose, and crossed to the washstand. He dumped the contents of the water pitcher over his head, dried himself, then picked up his hat and turned to Annie. "Anybody asks, I'm a helluva lover." He tossed four dollars into her lap and strode out.

Annie stared after him for an instant, then sank into a chair and began to cry softly.

Eleven

The mission was as silent and lonely as when McClain first saw it. He reined in beside the courtyard arch, dismounted, and tied his horse to the weathered hitch rack. He looked around soberly, remembering how Miguel had first described the place to him, struck by the accuracy of the priest's fond words. Even ravaged and neglected, the mission held an atmosphere of peace. In view of the violence which had taken place here, McClain wondered why this should be so, why, standing here, he should feel so strongly that he had reached a haven.

He wasn't an introspective man, but the staunch old building seemed a testimony to permanence, to patient strength in the face of assault. McClain realized suddenly that, in his own strange way, Miguel had the same kind of strength. It was a form of hope, just as the mission was. The place and the man had given McClain hope by forcing him to make a decision. For the moment he was no longer drifting. He had a goal. He was needed.

The gunfighter smiled wryly, thinking that Miguel had done him a favor by tricking him. Then he strode across the courtyard and entered the chapel.

McClain had not visited a holy place for many years. His gun had been his god and his salvation. He paused inside the battered door, removed his hat, and stood blinking in the gloom, filled with an unaccustomed deference.

As his eyes adjusted to the dimness, he saw that the chapel was plain, its rows of wooden benches crude, its stone walls without ornamentation. It should have been dismal, but the huge, oaken cross above the altar was polished to a gleaming brilliance which mirrored the flames of the candles beneath it, and seemed to illuminate everything it touched.

The thorn-crowned figure nailed to the cross was carved with exquisite care. Its pain-racked eyes held a lifelike quality, a wisdom as ancient as the stars. They sought McClain, seemed to speak to him.

The gunfighter stood motionless, inspired by this humble sanctuary. Then he became aware of a figure kneeling in the shadows before the altar. It was Miguel. He looked oddly unfamiliar in his priest's robe, his head bent in silent prayer.

McClain moved slowly up the aisle toward him. The priest heard his step and rose. Their

eyes met and held as McClain spoke quietly.
"Padre, I've come back to help."
"What changed your mind, my son?"
"Miss Annie Johnson."
Miguel's countenance lighted. "I told you she was a saint!"

Miguel's small room was behind the chapel. A chest, a cot, and a rough table near the hearth were its only furnishings. Seated at the table, bowls of thick soup before them, McClain repeated to Miguel the story that Annie had told him about the grave in the mission courtyard.

Miguel was stunned. "The grave is empty? A trick to make people believe I am dead? That is a dangerous hoax! The town will be in great peril if Lathrop discovers it!"

McClain shrugged. "Town deserves what it gets. But so far only four people know the truth – Annie, the mayor, that councilman fella, and the one that owns the boardinghouse. They ain't likely to do any tellin'."

Miguel pushed his soup aside, poured coffee, and began to pace restlessly. "So that is why the Indians called me *'diablo.'* They think I am damned because I broke my vow to them, that I have left my grave to do the Devil's bidding." Anguish twisted his features. "Poor souls! They have lost everything – even their faith." He met McClain's eyes urgently. "We must find a way to help them, my friend!"

"That's gonna take some doin'. Lathrop don't strike me as a man who lets go of *anything* easy."

Miguel nodded unhappy agreement. He returned to the table and sank into his chair thoughtfully. McClain had finished his soup and poured another cup of coffee before the priest's face brightened.

"Perhaps there is a way to renew their faith! It won't be easy, but it could succeed!"

McClain's eyes narrowed warily. "How can a devil give 'em faith?"

"We will prove to them that I am not a devil . . . that I am alive and have returned to free them."

"We? Meanin' just the two of us against Lathrop's bunch? That'll be quite a job, Padre. One I don't want any part of."

"You do not understand. We saw only part of the tribe at the mine. The fiercest warriors are still free. It was they who destroyed Lathrop's bullion wagon. Their chief is among those warriors."

"How d'you know that?"

"Each brave colors his weapons differently. I recognized the arrows and lances which destroyed the wagon." Miguel removed his priest's robe and hung it carefully on a wall peg. He was wearing his buckskins beneath it. "The warriors are undoubtedly hiding in the hills. We must find them and use them to help free the others."

McClain stared at him incredulously. "You'll never get within miles of 'em. Even warriors are scared of a devil!"

Miguel shoved his dagger into its sheath at his back. "That is true, but I will not be searching for them, my friend. *You* will be."

"Me? Like hell!"

"The braves need guns," explained Miguel calmly. "You have one. Therefore you will make an excellent decoy."

For an instant McClain was too dumbfounded to speak. Then he exploded indignantly. "Decoy! With savages, that's as good as *dead!*"

Miguel looked hurt. "Would a priest endanger his friend?"

"Maybe."

The priest shook his head sadly. "You still have no faith. I would go alone, but as you said, the Indians would be too fearful to show themselves."

"Well I don't aim to flush 'em out." McClain rose and reached for his hat.

"You said you had returned to help," reminded Miguel gently.

"Can't help by gettin' scalped."

"You will come to no harm. I promise. I have a plan."

McClain hesitated, frowning. "What kinda plan?"

Miguel smiled confidently, sensing the gunfighter's acquiescence. "Trust me, my friend. It is infallible. An inspiration from Heaven!"

Twelve

Nobody was greedier than Bart Lathrop. Even the generous veins of gold in the main tunnel of the tribal cave couldn't withstand the constant, rapacious gouging which had taken place during the six months since he took the cave away from the Indians. The "yellow rock" was beginning to run out.

Hungry for more, Lathrop kept the Indians working from dawn to dark, and ordered them to dig deeper into the hill in search of another vein. When they refused, insisting that scarring their sacred cave further would disturb its "medicine," he had them starved and lashed into obedience.

Now, although it was long past nightfall, he and four of his men stood just inside the cave entrance, watching the nervous prisoners hack a new tunnel in the rear wall. Dust and the flickering light of the guards' lanterns made it difficult to see and gave the atmosphere an eerie, dreamlike quality. The blows of pick and shovel echoed ominously, increasing the

Indians' uneasiness.

As the tunnel deepened, a faint, noxious odor became detectable. The Indians backed away, beginning to cough, and one of the guards called out to Lathrop.

"Smells like we hit a gas pocket, boss."

"Never mind. Just keep 'em digging!" yelled Lathrop.

Cursing and prodding, the guards forced the prisoners back to work. Suddenly their picks struck a jutting ledge of rock. It cracked and fell inward with a deep, growling rumble that brought part of the tunnel ceiling down with it. Rocks and debris filled the air, and an acrid cloud of poisonous gas mushroomed into the cave.

Shrieking and choking, the Indians scrambled out of the tunnel, dragging their chains with them, knocking the guards aside in their desperate flight.

Lathrop and his men backed from the cave, held the Indians just outside its entrance with shots and threats. Noses covered, the guards stumbled out to join Lathrop.

An uneasy hour passed. Then Lathrop took two of his men and reentered the mine. The air was clearing, even the smell of gas almost gone. Satisfied, the outlaw leader returned to the entrance.

"No gas inside now. Get the damn Indians

back to work," he ordered.

Converging on the prisoners, the guards prodded and lashed them toward the cave entrance. On the threshold, they huddled together, refusing to enter despite the guards' merciless blows.

"If we go in, we will be killed," cried one of the young warriors. "The spirits of the underworld are there. *Padre Diablo* has roused them against us!"

The other prisoners shrieked agreement and crowded back away from the cavern. They began chanting an eerie tribal supplication for protection against the Evil Ones.

The guards renewed their beatings, even fired shots into the air, but the Indians crouched on the ground, stubbornly unmovable, continuing their chant.

Frustrated, Lathrop ordered the guards to stop their punishment. He shouted grimly to the Indians, "We'll prove to you that the priest is dead. That his body is still in its grave!"

The Indians murmured uncertainly, their terror increased by his words. "If you open the ground, more evil spirits will come," cried an old man.

"There are no spirits! There's only a dead body!" Lathrop turned to his men. "Rafe, soon as it's light, you an' Hank ride to the mission. Dig up that damn priest and bring the body here so they can see it."

"Boss, that thing's really gonna stink!" Rafe grimaced with distaste.

"Hell with that! Bring it!"

Rafe exchanged an unhappy look with a bearded ruffian nearby. "Hope you got a strong stomach, Hank."

"Shut up or we'll be smellin' your bones!" Lathrop scowled at the two men for an instant, then turned back to the cowering Indians. "Your eyes will tell you what's true. You'll know that the priest is only coyote food. He can't hurt you or help you. Death will come only if you disobey *me!*"

The Indians stirred uneasily, glancing from Lathrop to the cave, equally terrified by both.

Thirteen

During the misty hush of the next morning's dawn, Miguel and McClain saddled up and left the mission. Tight-jawed and grim, once more wearing his buckskins, Miguel led the way swiftly to a hidden defile at the base of the hills that rimmed the plain. Its entrance was camouflaged by huge boulders so closely spaced that the two men had to dismount and lead their animals between them.

Beyond the boulders, the defile widened and climbed circuitously upward. Miguel stopped his mule and turned to the gunfighter, motioning toward the route ahead.

"Follow this wash. Soon you will find the trail which you must ride."

"Where does it go?" McClain's face was wary.

"It is the secret path to the tribal stronghold."

"Ridin' it won't get me a welcome."

"No. But it will force the warriors to contact you."

"Contact! You better make sure that's all they do!"

Miguel smiled confidently. "Have no fear, McClain. Heaven rides with you."

McClain snorted. "See that y'give Heaven a lotta help." He swung aboard his horse and jogged away along the defile. Miguel looked after him, murmuring soberly, "Heaven be with both of us, my friend."

Several miles of riding brought McClain to a faint, winding trail. He followed it, moving deeper and deeper into the hills. The canyons narrowed, growing increasingly dim, shadowy, and brush choked. There was no sign or sound of animal life, no rustling of insects or calling of birds. Only silence, deep and eerie. McClain felt as if he were riding through an empty world, on a path that had never been traveled. His horse stepped gingerly, body tense, as uneasy as his rider.

As the trail dropped away sharply into a deep ravine, the gunfighter halted. He was being watched. He could feel it . . . feel the hard, menacing probe of unfriendly eyes. He dropped a hand to his gun, loosened it in its holster, then urged his horse downward into the ravine.

The descent was boulder strewn and steep. Halfway down, the path had been washed away. A long slant of treacherous shale replaced it. Scrambling, McClain's horse hock-slid to the ravine's bottom and struggled for footing among rocks and sand.

It was then that they jumped him. Two Indian warriors materialized as if from nowhere, knives drawn, and knocked him from the saddle.

McClain lashed out with legs and arms, caught one man in the groin with a fierce blow that doubled him up, gasping. Tumbling backward, the gunfighter regained his feet just as the second warrior slashed with his knife. McClain gripped the man's wrist inches from its mark and twisted until a bone cracked. As the brave went to his knees, screaming, McClain pulled his gun. Before he could fire, the point of a spear pressed sharply against the small of his back and a gruff voice ordered him to drop his weapon. As he obeyed, three more husky braves converged on him, spears leveled.

They were different from the emaciated slaves the gunfighter had seen at Lathrop's mine, different from any Yaqui whom he had ever seen. These men were taller, cleaner limbed, with high-bridged noses and sharp features. Only their opaque black eyes and coppery skin marked them as of Indian origin.

McClain saw that their garb was also special. They wore pale deerhide leggings stained with colorful, abstract designs and their weapon belts were of soft, beaten gold. Each man's spear was feathered in individual color and arrangement. Clearly they were hardy men, filled with courage and pride.

The tallest of them wore a headband with a gleaming gold emblem on its front. Staring coldly at McClain, he drew his knife.

"Why you come here?" It was the same harsh voice McClain had heard before. "How you find this trail?"

McClain met the Indian's menacing gaze steadily. "I'm a trapper. Came lookin' for game."

The warrior studied him narrowly for a moment, then, "You speak lie. You are from Lathrop." He raised his knife, but before he could drive the blade into McClain's chest, Miguel's voice rang commandingly from the top of the ravine.

"No killing, my children! No killing!"

The Indians looked up, freezing with terror as they saw the priest descending toward them, his mule at a scrambling run. As he leaped to the ground beside McClain, they scattered, running for the opposite wall of the ravine, shrieking, *"Padre Diablo."*

Miguel threw McClain an anxious glance. "Are you injured, my friend?"

"No. But you were mighty slow gettin' here."

"I had to elude followers." Miguel crossed the ravine, shouting to the fleeing Indians, "Stop, my children! Stop or more evil will befall you!"

The Indians continued their flight, clawing toward the top of the ravine. McClain retrieved his gun and fired into the ground ahead of them. The bullets kicked up sprays of dirt and rock, striking almost at the Indians' feet.

The one wearing the headband halted, shouted to the others to do the same. As they obeyed, he turned slowly to face Miguel and McClain.

The priest strode to the base of the ravine wall and looked up at the frightened Indian leader.

"Yomuli, I am your friend. Do you not recognize me?"

"You from darkness. From evil." Yomuli's voice shook.

"No, I am Father Miguel, your priest."

"Priest dead. You devil spirit."

"I am alive. My flesh is warm. Come to me. I will prove it."

Yomuli backed away, shaking his head, his face convulsed with terror. "Touch of evil one brings death!"

Miguel drew the long knife from its sheath at his back and sliced a cruel gash in his forearm. As blood welled from the wound, he held his arm high.

"Do the dead bleed, Yomuli? Is the flesh of a devil warm?" The Indians exchanged startled exclamations.

"Come, Yomuli, taste my blood. Its warmth will prove that I live."

Commanding his braves to stay back, Yomuli descended warily to confront Miguel. Reaching out, he placed a finger against the priest's wound and realized wonderingly that the blood was indeed warm. Lifting the finger to his lips, he tasted.

Amazement flooded his features. "This man blood!" He called sharply to his braves. "Priest lives! Come, we make vengeance!"

Yomuli leveled his spear at Miguel's abdomen. The other braves surrounded the priest and McClain quickly, also with spears leveled.

Fourteen

Caught off guard by the Indians' sudden aggression, McClain and Miguel stood frozen in the circle of spears. Then Miguel scanned the faces of their grim captors with pained incredulity.

"You threaten your own priest, my children? It is a sin against Heaven!"

Yomuli's spear dug harder into Miguel's abdomen. "You no more our priest. Broke blood vow. Now people slaves. Sacred cave filled with evil spirits."

"I know, I know." Anguish roughened Miguel's voice. He pressed closer to the chief despite the thrusting spear. "Yomuli, I tried to die without speaking of the sacred cave and the yellow stones. But Lathrop's torture weakened my mind and loosened my tongue."

Contempt joined the hostility on Yomuli's face. "Man with heart of coyote not fit for priest."

"That is true." Miguel bowed his head in shamed acquiescence. "But even a coyote can help his brothers."

The chief's eyes blazed dangerously. "No more priest! No more brother!"

McClain murmured uneasily, "Hope you got more than talk up your sleeve, Padre. I don't hanker t'be a pincushion."

Miguel ignored him. He confronted Yomuli's rage desperately. "Lathrop's men left me for dead. By the will of Heaven, I lived – lived only to return and help free your people from their captivity. Now I am here and I have brought help."

For answer Yomuli spat at his feet. "You bring trouble! Since you come evil smoke fill cave, make Indians sick, blind eyes!"

"Your people will not work in the cave much longer. They will be free." Miguel gestured at McClain. "This man is a great gunwarrior. The outlaws fear his power. He will lead you and your braves against them." Yomuli's face remained closed, and Miguel's desperation increased. "Yomuli, you *must* believe me. I swear as your *blood brother* that I can help you."

The Indians murmured and exchanged glances, impressed by the priest's oath. Yomuli turned cold, appraising eyes on the gunfighter.

"If you have power, show us." He returned McClain's gun. "Shoot spear from sky, gunwarrior."

Holstering the weapon, McClain threw Miguel an accusing scowl. "Pray my *aim's* better'n your *plan.*"

He flexed his gun hand experimentally, grateful that the sun was high and hot. Then he tensed and nodded tightly to Yomuli.

The chief tossed his spear high. As it flattened and began its descent, McClain drew and fired. His bullet shattered the spear's shaft in midair.

Awed, the Indians grunted their admiration. Yomuli retrieved the shattered spear and examined it suspiciously. Satisfied that there was no trickery, he nodded brief approval at McClain, then turned to Miguel grimly.

"Gun-warrior's power is strong, but not mend priest's broken vow. Only death can mend."

Relief had begun to show on Miguel's face. Now it faded. "I remind the chief that under tribal law no man can be killed without a test of his guilt," he said carefully.

Yomuli seemed surprised. "You want 'test of truth'?"

"It is my right. I will prove that my vow was broken unwillingly and that I am still loyal to my blood bond."

The chief nodded solemnly. "Yomuli will test priest's truth. *To the death.*"

The listening braves murmured approval.

The chief handed his spear to one of them, removed his head badge, and drew his knife.

Miguel stripped off his shirt, revealing unexpectedly sinewy muscles and the broad chest more characteristic of a fighting man than a priest.

McClain noted this with astonishment which increased as Miguel accepted his knife from the brave who had taken it from him.

"You loco? You can't knife-fight an Injun!"

"It is against my beliefs, that is true. But I have no choice."

McClain stared at him disbelievingly. "Hell with your beliefs! He'll kill you!"

"If I do not fight him, we will *both* be killed, my friend." Their eyes met, a new, mutual respect and affection in the glance.

As Miguel strode to face Yomuli, the watching Indians widened their circle to give the two opponents more room. They took up a grim chant, drumming their spear shafts against the ground in accompaniment. The funereal rhythm sent chills along McClain's spine. He stiffened and set his teeth as Yomuli lunged suddenly at Miguel, his knife slicing toward the priest's chest.

Miguel ducked the blade and struck simultaneously with his own. Blood showed along Yomuli's ribs as the priest whirled to a position behind the chief.

The Indian spun quickly and lunged at Miguel with increased ferocity, his flashing knife driving the priest into a darting, backward dance to avoid it. Suddenly he stumbled and fell to his knees, losing his knife as he fought for balance.

Instantly Yomuli was on him. As he raised his weapon for a fatal plunge, Miguel gripped his wrist and threw himself backward, dragging Yomuli with him to the ground. The drumming spears and chanting rhythm increased as the two men rolled, struggling desperately for possession of the knife.

Watching, McClain felt perspiration stinging his armpits as Yomuli forced his weapon slowly downward toward Miguel's chest. The priest clung tenaciously to Yomuli's wrist, straining against the chief's brawny power.

McClain saw that it was a losing battle. He started forward. Two iron-handed braves jerked him sharply to a halt and held him motionless as the fight continued.

With the blade inches from his chest, Miguel suddenly jerked Yomuli's arm forward, twisting it cruelly in a movement that drove the chief's blade into the ground above Miguel's shoulder. With a mighty shove, the priest rolled his opponent aside and sprang to his feet. Before Yomuli could move, Miguel yanked the knife from the ground, straddled the chief, and placed the blade against his throat.

Abruptly, the Indians' chanting and drumming ceased. A tense silence replaced it as Miguel held the knife hard against Yomuli's throat. The chief waited for death, his eyes meeting the priest's unflinchingly.

At last Miguel spoke harshly. "I have passed the test of truth. I declare my vow mended, and claim Yomuli's loyalty to our blood vow."

"It is your right. Tribe will honor it."

"Good. It is also my right to spare the life of a blood brother. I claim it." Miguel lifted the knife from Yomuli's throat and rose to his feet.

With slow dignity, the chief stood to face him. He placed a hand on Miguel's shoulder. "My life now *your* life." His dark eyes were warm, filled with respect. He turned to his braves. "Hear chief's words. Our priest back. He speak. We listen."

Shouts of admiration and acceptance rose from the warriors' throats. They released McClain, returned his gun and Miguel's knife.

Now the priest announced that he had a plan which would enable them to defeat Lathrop's outlaws and free the rest of their tribe. Enthusiastically the Indians agreed to accompany Miguel and "the great gun-warrior" to the mission and to follow whatever instructions the priest gave them.

Riding back to the mission beside Miguel, McClain was silent and thoughtful. His attitude was in sharp contrast to the triumphant joviality of the accompanying Indians and the smiling relief of Miguel.

"You are very quiet, McClain. What is wrong?" asked the priest.

"I was just wonderin' how a priest got t'know so much about knife fightin'."

Miguel smiled wryly. "You see, my friend, I came late to the priesthood."

"You broke a passel of vows today."

"Broke? On the contrary, I fulfilled them."

McClain gave him a skeptical look. "With a pigsticker?"

"Religion is practiced in many ways." Miguel's voice was patient. "The 'test of truth' is part of the ancient Yaqui religion. By utilizing it, I was able to do my priestly duty."

McClain glared at him indignantly. "How d'you figure *that?*"

"By fighting, I prevented two deaths, yours and mine. Such prevention is a part of my vows, not a violation." Miguel smiled ingenuously. "You see, my friend, how simple it is?"

"No! And I got a feelin' I never will!" Exasperated, the gunfighter put spurs to his horse and galloped ahead.

Fifteen

At the mission the "grave" of Father Miguel lay open to the mid-morning sun, its marker half buried in the mountain of dirt beside it. Rafe and Hank stood on opposite sides of the excavation, hauling on ropes, straining to lift a crude wooden coffin to the surface.

As they worked, a horseman jogged slowly to a halt just inside the mission courtyard. He slouched in the saddle, unkempt, with a shapeless, sweat-stained hat pulled low against the sun and a shiny gun hung loosely on his thigh. There was a go-to-hell arrogance in his manner that contrasted sharply with his nondescript appearance. He sat watching the two men as the coffin rose slowly and cleared the pit at last.

With a final, Herculean pull, Rafe and Hank dragged it to level ground. They straightened, panting, tensed as they saw the horseman. "Who are you, kid? What's your business here?" Rafe stepped toward the stranger belligerently.

"Name's Hal Peters." The words came patronizingly from smirking lips. "An' my business ain't none of yours."

Rafe scowled and dropped his hand to the side of his holster. "Then mosey and forget you stopped."

"Pull that iron an' *you'll* forget everything."

Rafe started to retort, stopped sharply as sun glinted on the gold shamrock dangling from the kid's neck. His glance slid from the gold to the gun on Peters's hip, and he moved his hand carefully away from his holster.

"No need for trouble, kid."

Peters grinned mockingly. "Not till I find what I'm lookin' for."

"Which is bullets, for sure," remarked Hank dryly.

"I been trailin' a broken-down gunny called Glint McClain. Either of ya' seen him?"

Hank studied Peters curiously. "Heard about him. You want bullets, he'll have 'em."

Peters scowled, and Rafe gave Hank a warning glance. "Saw McClain yesterday. In Rileyville."

"Where's that?" Peters asked sharply.

"Three miles north."

Peters whirled his horse and galloped away, spurring hard.

Rafe and Hank stared after him. "Sure proddy," remarked Hank.

"You see that gold neck piece he was wearin'?"

Hank nodded. "Yeah. Why?"

"Look like a shamrock t'you?"

"Never seen a shamrock."

"Neither did I. Except on Glint McClain," mused Rafe.

Hank shrugged. "So?"

"He claimed it was lucky. Never took it off."

Hank turned toward the coffin, disinterested in further speculation. "We totin' the whole box or just what's inside?"

Rafe abandoned his musings reluctantly. "Body's enough."

"It'll stink more."

"Weigh less."

Hank sighed. "Just so we keep it downwind."

They tugged at the coffin lid. It lifted crookedly and slid backward to the ground. The two men stared down at a jumble of rocks and sand, shock growing on their faces.

Sixteen

At the mine the Indians were receiving their noon ration of water. Chained in the dirt near the cave entrance, without escape from the sun's relentless heat, they reached eagerly for the meager dippers of liquid which the guards were passing out. Their cries for more were answered with kicks and blows.

Lathrop paced restlessly nearby, pausing often to scan the trail leading toward the mission. The other members of his band lounged in the shade of several jutting boulders, consuming beans and coffee, ignoring the hungry glances of the Indians.

A scraping sound and the thud of jogging hooves brought the outlaws to their feet. A moment later, Rafe and Hank rode into view. Miguel's "coffin," tied with ropes, bumped and dragged behind their lathered horses. They hauled it closer, released it near the cave, and dismounted wearily. At the sight of the coffin, the Indians rose and backed away, murmuring with fear.

Lathrop greeted the riders scowlingly. "Took long enough gettin' back. What held you up?"

Rafe jerked a thumb at the coffin. "Thing's heavy. Took a lotta liftin' and a lotta draggin'."

"Heavy! A pine box with some bones in it?"

Hank loosened the ropes, threw back the coffin's lid, and scooped out a handful of its contents. "No bones. Just these, boss."

As Lathrop and his men stared incredulously, the Indians began to shriek.

"Grave empty!" yelled a brave. *"Padre Diablo* walks! Evil comes!"

The Indians' hysteria increased. They milled around, tugging frantically at their chains.

"Shut 'em up!" yelled Lathrop to the guards. "Shut 'em up!"

The two guards converged on the prisoners, beating them until they quieted and huddled to the ground, moaning their terror.

Lathrop pawed at the coffin's contents with mounting fury, turned accusingly on Hank and Rafe. "You sure you got the right grave?"

"Had the priest's marker on it," replied Hank sullenly.

Lathrop's rage increased. "That mayor an' his yokels made fools of us. Musta helped the priest escape, then rigged the grave so we'd think he was dead."

"An' all this time they been laughin' at us," agreed Rafe.

"Well, the joke's over. We'll fix it so they're laughin' on the other side of their faces!" Lathrop shouted to his men. "Mount up!"

As the outlaws hurried to their horses, Lathrop turned to the guards.

"No more water for those damn savages till they go back to work!" He swung aboard his horse and galloped off toward town, his men following.

Seventeen

Rileyville dozed tranquilly in the early afternoon sun. Here and there a scattering of townspeople moved unhurriedly along the boardwalk, bent on various mundane errands. They glanced curiously at Hal Peters as he jogged down the dusty street. He halted beside a drunk who sprawled on the ground, snoring spasmodically, his head propped against a pole of the saloon hitch rail.

Peters dismounted, rolled the drunk aside with a rough shove of his boot, and tethered his animal. Bellied in the dirt, the drunk lay blinking after him groggily as he strode toward the batwings.

The saloon was mildly busy. Several ranchers stood at the bar talking. Four other men played poker at a nearby table, and in a rear corner Annie sat with an ardent young wrangler, enduring his advances wearily.

Peters shoved through the doors and surveyed the gathering, arrogant, his glance sharp and searching. His manner drew attention.

Slowly the room fell silent, all eyes on his aggressive figure and his low-slung gun.

Peters returned their scrutiny challengingly, announcing, "I want Glint McClain. Where do I find him?"

The ranchers and poker players shook their heads blankly, but Annie's face whitened. She pulled away from her companion, exchanged a tense glance with the bartender.

Peters noticed their reaction. Instantly his gun was out and leveled at the bartender. "Talk, mister!"

"He was here yesterday. Said he was just passin' through," replied the barman nervously.

"Passin' through to where?"

"Didn't say." The bartender nodded toward the rear table. "Just bought a bottle and went upstairs with Annie."

Peters turned toward the girl. She shook her head uneasily. "He . . . he didn't do much talkin'."

"You're lyin'!" Peters moved toward her ominously.

Annie rose, clutched the back of her chair for support. "No! Honest, mister! Honest!"

His free hand shot out and cracked against her cheek. "Where is he? *Where?*"

The blow brought tears to Annie's eyes and left an angry red stain across her cheek. She swayed for an instant, then steadied, her eyes hardening.

"He *paid* me not t'say. You pay, too."

For an instant Peters's eyes blazed. Then he swore contemptuously, "Greedy whore!" He tossed a silver dollar to the table. "Talk!"

Annie picked up the coin and dropped it into her bosom, eyes still hard and unreadable. "He mentioned Cedar Mesa . . . somethin' about meetin' a friend."

Peters studied her narrowly for a moment, then holstered his gun. "I don't find him, I'll be back." He slapped her again, harder, then strode out of the saloon.

Annie sank into her chair and poured herself a drink as the young wrangler slid a comforting arm around her shoulders.

"Bastard!" he said. "Hope this McClain shoots his balls off." He studied Annie curiously for an instant, then asked, "Lied for him, didn't ya?"

Annie nodded.

"How come?"

"It wasn't for him. It was for somebody else." She downed her drink, shakily poured another.

Outside, Peters mounted his horse and loped toward the far edge of town. As dust misted his disappearing figure, Lathrop and his men thundered into view, firing as they came.

They skidded to a halt in the center of the street, milling around, still firing into the air and shouting to the townspeople to come out.

Slowly doors opened and the frightened inhabitants emerged. They gathered tensely near the saloon. The outlaws circled them, herding them to face Lathrop.

"Where's your mayor?" His eyes raked the small crowd. "And that Chairman Fowler? Get 'em out here!"

Jake Gulden and two hefty ranchers hurried into a nearby building. They reappeared a few minutes later hauling Mayor Spencer and Chairman Fowler with them. The crowd parted, allowing them to shove the unhappy pair to the side of Lathrop's horse.

He looked down at them contemptuously. "Well, seems like the town leaders don't wanna give us a welcome, boys."

His men laughed raucously.

"They act like they're hidin' somethin', boss," suggested Rafe.

Lathrop's cold gaze impaled the two uneasy men. "You figure it could have somethin' to do with that *dead* priest?"

Fowler and Spencer tensed, fighting to hide their increasing fear. The mayor was the first to regain a degree of composure.

"We have nothing to hide, Lathrop. Nothing at all."

"You lyin' skunk! You heard the Indians talk about a devil ghost. They been seein' him for three days. They're so scared they won't work!"

The mayor swallowed nervously. "All Indians are superstitious. Surely you don't believe their talk!"

Fury contorted Lathrop's face. Leaning over, he slashed Spencer viciously with his long romal. "They're not seein' ghosts. They're seein' the priest, Father Miguel. He's still alive an' your people helped him stay that way!"

The townspeople gasped and shouted frightened denials, but Lathrop refused to accept them. Shouting angrily, he revealed that his men had opened the grave at the mission and found it filled with rocks, he accused the town of trickery, of deliberately helping Father Miguel to escape.

"We're not to blame," yelled a rancher. "If the priest's alive, it ain't our doin'."

"Maybe not," retorted Lathrop grimly, "but I'm holdin' all of you responsible. I'm givin' you twelve hours to find him an' bring him to me. I don't care if he's *dead* or *alive*. Just so he can't stir up the Indians!"

"How can we find him?" asked the mayor desperately. "We don't know where he's hiding!"

"Find out! Bring him to the mission in twelve hours or we'll burn the town to the ground!" Spinning his horse, Lathrop galloped away in the direction of the mine. His men followed, shooting out windows and watering troughs as their parting warnings.

Eighteen

As the mission came into sight across the sun-drenched plain, Miguel signaled the Indians and McClain to halt. He studied the silent courtyard carefully, then sent two of Yomuli's best scouts ahead to make sure its apparent desertion held no ambush.

They slipped from their horses, scurried forward, and dropped to their bellies. Separating, they melted into the landscape and approached the mission from opposite directions, as indistinguishable as grains of sand.

Long, voiceless moments passed. Then the chapel doors opened. A scout emerged and signaled all-clear with raised spear. An instant later his companion sprang lightly into view on the courtyard wall, also raising his spear.

Relieved, Miguel led the party into the mission courtyard. As the Indians concealed his mule and their own mounts behind the chapel, Miguel conferred with Yomuli.

"Place watchers on the walls, Yomuli, and tell your braves to move carefully. If our plan is to succeed, we must not be seen."

As the chief nodded and strode toward several waiting warriors, McClain spoke dryly from behind the priest.

"Afraid it's too late for secrets, Padre."

Miguel turned. McClain stood several feet away, beside the opened gravesite. The priest strode to his side. He looked from the empty pit to the pile of dirt beside it with stunned comprehension.

"Lathrop must have become suspicious! Only *he* would have reason to do this thing!"

"Figures. He ain't the kind t'believe in devils."

Miguel scooped a handful of soil from inside the cavity and examined it. "The earth is still damp. The grave has not been open long."

"Two . . . maybe three hours," agreed McClain, "but that's long enough t'start 'em lookin' for you."

Miguel nodded thoughtfully, dusted soil from his hands, and straightened. "We must hurry the plan, McClain. Ride into town at once. Alert the men. We will need them."

"And if they won't listen to me?"

"They will listen. Lathrop is no fool." Miguel motioned at the grave. "He will blame the town for its trickery. Already he will have threatened vengeance if the people do not produce me."

"So they'll turn you over to him!"

"I have taken that possibility into consideration, McClain."

"An' you're still willin' t'stick your neck out?"

Miguel stared at him, eyes lighting. "My *neck?* That is an interesting thought, my friend. I am glad you mentioned it."

McClain scowled. "I'd feel easier if I knew more about this plan."

"It is not yet complete."

"Not complete!? Then how d'you know it'll work?"

"I do not, but *Heaven* does. It will show me the way, as always."

"Just see to it I'm not the bait again." McClain strode away.

Miguel looked after him with an enigmatic smile. "You will not be, my friend. That I promise," he murmured.

Nineteen

In Rileyville, fear trapped the people like a rising flood tide, washing away the veneer of civilization to expose the gritty sands of venom, cowardice, and inhumanity.

Crowded around the steps of the saloon, the inhabitants confronted Mayor Spencer and Councilman Fowler angrily.

"You mean t'say we buried an empty coffin?" demanded a rancher.

"We knew it was a risk, Ben. We thought it was safer if only a few of us knew about it." Spencer faced the crowd unhappily from the top of the steps.

"That won't cut any leather with Lathrop," retorted the rancher.

The townsfolk shouted agreement, and a cowpoke yelled furiously that Rileyville wouldn't be in danger if Father Miguel had been allowed to die.

"That no-good priest's not worth this risk," screamed a woman hysterically. "I got children t'think of! And a ranch!"

The discussion continued with increasing savagery and brutal agreement that Miguel must be found, the town saved from destruction at any cost.

"He's probably hidin' out with the Indians. They'll never let us find him!" called a man. "They'll burn the town out, an' we've got our mayor t'thank for it!"

There were shouts of agreement, and a husky wrangler shoved Spencer roughly against the saloon wall.

"You got us into this, Spencer. Now get us out. Where'd he be likely t'hide?"

"How do I know? He promised never to come back. That's the only reason we helped him!" Spencer was white with fear.

"Anybody knows where he is, it's that whore Annie," shrieked a middle-aged ranch wife. "They was lovers!"

"That's a lie!" Annie emerged from behind the saloon's swinging doors, where she had been listening. Anger lent her courage. "He was my friend. Only one I ever had. That's why I nursed him, an' I'm proud of it!"

"She's lyin'!" screamed the ranch wife. "She'll protect him if we all die for it!"

"You're all cowards an' hypocrites! I wouldn't tell you anything if I knew it!" Annie's voice trembled with emotion.

"Come on! Let's beat it out of her!" The ranch wife lunged at Annie, slapping her and pulling her hair. Several more women joined the attack. Annie fought back, kicking and biting, but they knocked her to the ground, striking her repeatedly. The men watched, urging the women on, shouting ugly names at Annie.

The tumult of assault drowned the sound of hoofbeats as McClain galloped into view from the end of the street. His horse slid to a halt at the fringe of the gathering.

A mixture of consternation and fury washed across his features as he saw Annie, bloodied and half-naked, on the ground.

"Let her go!" He jerked out his gun and fired several shots into the air. "Dammit, let her go!"

Startled, the crowd looked toward him, grew silent, the frenzied women releasing Annie. All emotions locked by the gunplay.

"Now get outa my way!"

As the crowd wavered, then separated, McClain dismounted and helped Annie to her feet. She clung to him weakly, tears streaking the blood on her cheeks.

"They want Father Miguel. They tried t'make me tell where he is."

McClain's gaze raked the gathering contemptuously. "So your damn town's worth more than a man's life. Bunch of boards an' glass. I don't know what you are, but you're sure not human! A coyote's got more balls than any man here!"

The men stirred shamefacedly, but the ranch wife was unabashed. "Easy talk, mister. It ain't your town or your life."

The gunfighter's contempt increased. "You can stop worryin' about your precious lives. I'll take you to the priest."

He put an arm around Annie and helped her into the saloon as the crowd murmured with relieved astonishment. Inside, he seated her at a table, got a bottle from behind the bar, and poured her a drink. As she gulped it down gratefully, he asked, "You gonna be all right?"

She nodded, eyes searching his face urgently, "You go on. Father's gonna need you."

"You get some rest." McClain started for the door.

Annie's voice stopped him. "Hope you know what you're doin', McClain."

He turned to look at her reassuringly. "Only partly, but Miguel's got a plan."

Their eyes met with a mixture of understanding and apprehension. Then McClain strode outside.

The town men were mounted and waiting. "Where we headed?" asked one.

The gunfighter gave him a cold look. "Just follow me."

Putting spurs to his horse, he galloped away. The men followed, choking on his dust.

Twenty

Crouched atop the mission's front walls, unmoving and undetectable except to the practiced eye, two of Yomuli's braves scanned the surrounding desert. Through the silver haze of afternoon sunlight, a group of horsemen became visible, approaching at a high lope.

One sentry turned and gave a soft, chirping signal to the brave standing silently at the chapel doors. The brave answered with a similar signal, then disappeared, wraithlike, into the chapel. The braves on the walls dropped lightly to the mission courtyard and melted to invisibility amidst its brush and debris.

Moments later, the horsemen galloped into the courtyard, McClain leading. The party dismounted, the townsmen looking around at the apparent desertion suspiciously.

"Don't look like anybody's here. Where's the priest?" demanded the rancher named Ben belligerently.

"Just follow me," snapped McClain. "He's

waitin' for you." He mounted the chapel steps.

"Follow, hell! Let's take him, boys," shouted the rancher. Rifle in hand, he started for the steps, the others crowding behind him.

McClain whirled, drawing his gun with a swift motion. He faced them, weapon leveled, eyes as cold as its steel barrel. "First man that moves is dead."

As the townsmen halted, taken aback by the gunfighter's swift proficiency, the two Indian sentries materialized on opposite sides of the party, their spears leveled.

"Yomuli's braves!" The consternation in the mayor's voice echoed that on his companions' faces. He turned accusingly on McClain. "What is this? I thought you were a stranger to these parts, McClain!"

"I am, Mayor. But since we met, I took a job."

"Gunslingin' for who?"

McClain smiled grimly. "Father Miguel." He enjoyed the men's stunned alarm for a moment, then ordered, "Now drop your guns."

"Hold on, fella, we –"

The gunfighter's flinty gaze cut Ben's words short. "I said drop your guns."

The men dropped their guns reluctantly.

"Now follow me. An' remember . . . you're

goin' t'church." McClain led them into the chapel. The Indian sentries followed, their spears ensuring that the group remained intact.

Twenty-One

Father Miguel, wearing his priest's robes, stood at the foot of the altar flanked by Yomuli and his braves. The chapel was alight with candles. Their flickering glow etched the statuesque Indians and their priest with gold and cast their images in gigantic shadows on the walls.

Entering behind McClain, the townsmen hesitated, awed by the compelling tableau and the hushed authority which pervaded the long, narrow room.

McClain crossed to the priest, took a place beside him, his manner leaving no doubt as to his allegiance. Cautious and uncomfortable, the townsmen approached to confront Miguel.

"I see that you have come for me, gentlemen. No doubt at Lathrop's bidding." The priest spoke with quiet dignity.

The townsmen's discomfiture increased. For a moment they evaded Miguel's probing eyes.

Then the mayor replied defensively, "We

told you not to come back. You should've listened."

"To listen was to remain a coward, to leave my people in slavery."

"Nobody can help the Indians, or you either. Not now."

"Because Lathrop wants me dead?" There was an undercurrent of challenge in Miguel's tone.

Ben answered with equal challenge. "Right! An' it's either you or the town."

Miguel looked from Ben's grim eyes to the faces of the others. All held a mixture of fear and determination. Sorrow swept the priest's features.

"You are as weak as I was, my friends. To ensure your own safety, you have ignored the misfortunes of other human beings. That is my fault. I should not have allowed it to happen. As a priest, it was my duty to act against evil, no matter where it existed. Instead, I waited until it was directed against me."

The men exchanged shamed looks, torn by his words but still dominated by fear of Lathrop's outlaws.

Miguel sensed their feelings and spoke with increased urgency. "Evil has dominated you too long. It is time for your people and Yomuli's to unite against it."

"Unite!" cried Ben. "Ranchers and a bunch

of Indians with spears! What chance'd we have against Lathrop's gunfighters?"

"He's right," yelled a wrangler, "an' we ain't dyin' for a tribe of heathens! Or for you either, priest!" He lunged at Miguel, halted sharply as he found two spears against his belly. He glared at the priest.

"You got the drop on us now, but y'can't keep it like this. You gotta let us loose or tomorrow you'll be facin' Lathrop *and* us!"

His companions murmured agreement, their attitudes a mixture of hostility and guilt. Miguel studied them sadly, perceiving their emotions. After a silent moment, he pointed out that if they murdered him, as Lathrop demanded, they would take on the evil which the outlaws offered. They would be killers, just as Lathrop and his men were and having shed innocent blood, they would never escape its stain. Even more, they would need to kill McClain and also Yomuli's people because they would be witnesses to their actions.

"Murder is never an end, my friends," said the priest. "It is the beginning of inner torment, the death not only of the victim, but of the killer's soul."

The townsmen exchanged glances, disturbed by his commanding words and compelling authority.

Miguel's eyes searched their faces urgently.

"I offer you a choice, my friends. A lifetime of fear and guilty pretense, or the courage to fight for the life you had before these outlaws came to terrorize you."

The men conferred, almost convinced by the priest's plea but uneasy about their chances of success against Lathrop's band.

Miguel brushed aside their doubts, pointed out that united with Yomuli's people, the town inhabitants outnumbered the outlaws. He added that none of Lathrop's men was as fast a gun as Glint McClain, and the outlaws would recognize that danger.

"Furthermore, there will be no need for actual fighting. You see, I have a plan which will accomplish our success without bloodshed."

"What kinda plan?" asked Ben dubiously.

Miguel smiled at the gathering with benign confidence. "A foolproof one, my friends. All you have to do is arm yourselves and trust me." He was a silver-tongued savior now, and he held their hopes in the palm of his hand.

The mayor scanned his companions' faces. "Well, what do you say, boys?"

Impressed by the priest's assurance, the men found new courage.

"Guess anything's better'n murder," offered Ben.

"Long as there won't be no shootin'," agreed a wrangler.

The mayor turned to Miguel. "All right, Father, we'll go along with you."

"Just tell us what t'do, Padre." The cowpoke's voice held a new deference.

"When and where are you to deliver me to Lathrop?" asked Miguel.

"They'll be coming for you at noon tomorrow. Here," replied Spencer.

"I will be waiting for them at the courtyard gate," smiled Miguel.

Everyone stared at him, startled. "They're liable t'shoot you on sight, Padre!" warned a rancher.

"Do not fear, my friends. Heaven will protect me," the priest declared serenely.

"Long as there won't be no shootin'," warned a [illegible].

The mayor turned to Miguel. "All right Father, we'll go along with you."

"Just tell us what to do, Padre." The compadre's voice held a new deference.

"When and where are you to deliver him to Lathrop?" asked Miguel.

"They'll be coming for you, or leastwise for [illegible]," replied Spencer.

"I will be waiting for them at the courtyard gate," smiled Miguel.

"Everyone [illegible] at [illegible] Miguel. "They're liable [illegible] you [illegible], Padre!" warned a [illegible].

"Do not [illegible] any [illegible]. [illegible] will go [illegible] and [illegible]," the priest declared serenely.

Twenty-Two

The following morning was chill and somber. It remained so, with dank clouds and a drifting mist obscuring the midday sun when Lathrop and his men appeared on a rise overlooking the mission.

Bunched together, grim-faced and gun-heavy, they made an ominous tableau as they reined in, eyes raking the landscape suspiciously.

The mission appeared unchanged to them, a silent, decaying ghost.

Rafe squinted, trying to see through the mist. "Don't see anybody. They should be waitin' for us."

Hank leaned forward in his saddle, gaze sharpening. "What's that hangin' from the gate? See it, boss?"

Lathrop raised a spyglass and focused it on the courtyard entrance. It revealed a dark-robed figure dangling from the gate's arch by a hangman's rope. Lathrop scrutinized the figure with growing astonishment, then lowered the glass and shouted triumphantly to the others.

"It's the priest! They've hanged him!"

Yelling exultantly, the band galloped forward. They burst into the deserted courtyard and milled to a noisy stop, leaping from their saddles. As they started toward the swinging figure, a volley of spears and arrows whizzed past their heads. The quivering shafts dug into the ground ahead, forming a warning barrier between them and the gate. As they froze, Yomuli and his braves rose from concealment on the chapel roof. A warrior raised his bow and sent another arrow speeding toward the courtyard gate. It severed the rope above the black-robed figure. Miguel dropped to the ground lightly and removed the loosely draped noose from his neck, revealing that it was a fake. Tossing off his robes, he removed another rope which passed under his armpits, enabling him to "hang" without injury.

He grinned at the stunned outlaws impudently. "You seem surprised, *bandidos*. Have you never heard of a 'stage noose'?"

As he spoke, the men of Rileyville showed themselves on the courtyard walls, their guns and rifles leveled. Tensely the outlaws assessed the situation and realized that they were completely surrounded.

Lathrop yelled desperately, "Let's ride, boys!" He dove for his horse. The others did the same.

Spears and arrows streaked from above to pierce the ground between them and the animals. The horses reared and scattered, dashing past the frustrated outlaws.

Miguel's voice whirled them around. He stood among the men on the walls now. "You are trapped, Lathrop. It would be wise to surrender."

Lathrop glared contemptuously at the surrounding townsmen. "You can't hold us. You're too lily-livered t'shoot!"

"Do not underestimate us, Lathrop. We will not let you go," advised Miguel grimly.

Pretending to consider the priest's warning, Lathrop spoke softly to his men. "Start shootin', boys. We'll make a run for the chapel."

He jerked out his gun and snapped a shot at Miguel. It grazed the priest's cheek. As Miguel dropped to cover, Lathrop's companions raced for the mission doors, firing at their captors as they ran.

Spears and arrows flew, rifles spoke, but the outlaws disappeared into the chapel unharmed, leaving two wounded townsmen behind them.

Gathered in the small adobe cook shack behind the mission, Spencer, Ben, and several other ranchers conferred while Miguel cleaned and dressed the wounds of the two injured townsmen. He seemed unaware of the blood welling from his own wound. McClain, seated in a chair tilted against the wall, kept a watchful eye on the window that overlooked the rear courtyard of the mission.

"You said there'd be no bloodshed, Padre." There was accusation in Spencer's voice.

"I did not think Lathrop would be so unwise."

"Might not have happened if you'd let 'em see McClain was with us."

"Keeping him unseen was part of my plan," responded the priest. He glanced at the others reassuringly. "Do not worry, *compadres*. Their bullets accomplished nothing."

"Knocked out two of our guns," remarked McClain dryly.

"The men are not badly hurt, and we no longer need so many guns."

McClain threw him a skeptical look. "How come? Lathrop's bunch has been holed up in that chapel all day. Can't be too comfortable. They're bound t'try another breakout, and a hard one."

Miguel shook his head, undisturbed. "Perhaps. But from now on, *your* gun will be our shield, McClain. That is the other part of my plan."

"Should've figured *I'd* get the trouble part."

"The path to justice is seldom easy, my friend." The priest completed bandaging and doused his bloodied face in a nearby basin of water. He mopped it dry with a ragged towel and turned toward the door.

"And now, *compadres,* I will speak to Lathrop about *his* plan."

The others frowned bewilderedly. "How d'you know he's got one?" Ben queried.

Miguel grinned wickedly. "If he has not, I shall *induce* one. Watch for my signal, McClain." He opened the door a crack, peered out to make sure the way was clear, then raced toward the courtyard wall.

Twenty-Three

Crouching, Miguel raced to a crude wooden ladder fitted into a niche of the courtyard's side wall. Yomuli's warriors and the guarding townsmen covered his progress. He moved swiftly along the narrow walkway at the top of the wall to a position opposite the chapel doors. Shielded behind a raised section of the wall's inner bulwark, he shouted loudly to the outlaw leader.

"Come out, Lathrop! You will not be harmed. We wish to parley." There was no reply. Miguel shouted again, "I give you my word as a priest. You will be safe."

For a moment there was only silence. Then the chapel door opened a few inches, and Lathrop called harshly.

"Show yourself, priest. I'll come out when you do."

The townsman standing near Miguel shook his head in sharp negation. "Don't do it, Padre. They'll cut y'down!"

"If they do, stand firm. Do not allow them

to escape. There is too much at stake." Miguel raised an arm, signaling to Yomuli's braves and the surrounding townsmen to cover him. Then he dropped to the ground.

"I am out, Lathrop. Come and meet me!" He strode boldly to the center of the courtyard.

Slowly Lathrop emerged from the chapel. Three men with leveled rifles accompanied him. He paused at the top of the steps, glancing around tensely at the grim guardians on the walls.

"Closer, Lathrop! It is difficult to parley while shouting."

Lathrop descended the steps uneasily and advanced to within a few feet of Miguel. "Anybody shoots, you're dead, priest."

"No one will shoot. We wish to avoid further bloodshed. Your surrender will accomplish that."

Lathrop scowled. "We'll see you in hell first!"

"Your attitude is foolish," pointed out Miguel. "You cannot escape. There are too many of us against you."

"Maybe. But my men are better shots. And they don't *mind* killin'. The ranchers *do*, and they hate the idea of dyin'."

"Even so, they will never permit you to escape."

"When the shootin' starts again, they'll change their minds," Lathrop declared smugly.

"We can starve you out."

"Try it. There'll be shootin' all the way."

"Your bullets may be more accurate than ours, but they will not protect you from flames."

Lathrop stared at him, appalled, "You'd let 'em burn your mission? You're bluffin'!"

Their eyes locked. Miguel's were cold as death. "We will burn it to the ground – with you in it if necessary."

Lathrop whitened, reading the iron determination in the priest's face. Miguel studied him narrowly, sensing that he had won an advantage.

"As I said, we would prefer to avoid violence. If you could suggest a compromise, perhaps even a mutual gamble . . ."

"You mean like a bet, an' if we won, you'd let us go?" Lathrop asked shrewdly.

"We would escort you out of the territory."

Lathrop considered for a moment, then suggested slyly, "You willin' to risk a two-man shoot-out?"

A flicker of triumph showed briefly on Miguel's face. "You suggest a duel?"

"You could call it that," said Lathrop. "One of my boys against anybody you want."

Miguel seemed shocked. "But more blood would be shed!"

"One dead man's better than a bunch."

"That is true." Miguel weighed the idea for a moment, then asked, "And if the dead man is yours, you will surrender peacefully?"

Lathrop smirked. "That's right."

"And you will accept any champion we name?" asked Miguel insistently.

"That's what I said."

The priest hesitated, then nodded. "Very well, we have an agreement."

Lathrop's eyes gleamed with the cunning conviction that he had suckered the priest into a losing bargain. "Who's your man?"

Miguel raised an arm in signal to the men on the walls. In response, McClain appeared from behind a section of the bulwark, showing himself among them for the first time.

"Name's McClain," he called, "Glint McClain." He dropped to the ground and crossed to Miguel's side.

Lathrop stared at him, dismayed. His feelings were echoed in the faces of his three backup men on the steps of the chapel. As comprehension dawned, the outlaw leader turned furiously on Miguel.

"You slimy sidewinder! You foxed me in!"

Miguel seemed taken aback. "You agreed to accept any man chosen."

"You didn't say y'had Glint McClain. None of my boys'll draw against *him!*"

The bewilderment on Miguel's face increased. "But your followers are experienced gunmen. All of them!"

"Too experienced t'draw against McClain. The deal's off!"

Both men looked up as a strange male voice called sharply from just outside the courtyard gate.

"I'll draw against him!"

Smugly aware that all attention was centered on him, Hal Peters rode into the courtyard and dismounted. Twirling McClain's lucky piece in his fingers, he swaggered to Lathrop's side.

"Took this off him when I gunned him down before," he boasted, looking insolently at McClain. "Been trailin' him for days. Came t'finish what I started back at the stream, McClain."

Miguel and McClain exchanged a glance, both acutely aware of the drifting mist and the chill of approaching dusk.

"Been expectin' you. Call your time and place." The gunfighter kept his tone even, without sign of the uncertainty he was feeling.

"How about right now?"

Miguel spoke hastily. "No, it will soon be dark. The contest must take place in full daylight so that everyone can see it clearly and be sure that it is completely fair."

Peters scowled. "I ain't waitin' around all night for –"

Miguel interrupted him coldly, gesturing at the surrounding townsmen and Indians. "You will wait, Peters, or there will be no duel. *My* people are making the rules!"

Twenty-Four

The night was inky and starless, punctuated by the low rumble of distant thunder. A mist-veiled moon played hide-and-seek with drifting clouds, and dampness hung heavily in the air, adding to its chill.

Both townsmen and Indians guarded the mission walls, but the courtyard was deserted and only a flicker of lantern light showed from within the chapel to acknowledge the presence of those inside.

A large fire blazed just outside of the courtyard walls. Yomuli and his braves clustered around it, the warriors helping themselves to the aromatic contents of a caldron of meat simmering above the flames. Their talk was intermittent, subdued by reflections on the day's grim events and somber anticipation of what the morning would bring.

McClain stood with hands outstretched to the fire's warmth, flexing his fingers experimentally. Miguel hunkered beside him, a worried frown creasing his forehead as the gunfighter grimaced with discomfort.

"Fingers are stiff as a sweaty cinch. No way I can outdraw Peters if it don't warm up."

Miguel nodded unhappily. "I am sorry, my friend. I did not anticipate *his* arrival."

The gunfighter shrugged. "Can't be helped. I just hope tomorrow's sunny an' warm."

Miguel rose and placed a hand on McClain's shoulder. "I shall pray for it, my friend," he said fervently, "with all my soul."

He strode away into the darkness. From the opposite side of the fire, Yomuli looked after him, concerned by his troubled attitude. After a moment, the chief rose and slipped into the night, moving in the direction taken by Miguel.

He found the priest on a sandy rise. He knelt, rosary in hand, face turned to the heavens, praying silently. Yomuli moved to him soundlessly and waited until Miguel became aware of his presence.

Then he asked softly, "Why does priest kneel alone with empty heart?"

"I have done a wrong thing, Yomuli. I have endangered the life of a man who trusted me."

"What man?"

"The gun-warrior whom I brought to help us."

The bewilderment on Yomuli's face increased. "Gun-warrior not die. His medicine strong like shield. He kill stranger."

Miguel shook his head sadly. "He has a sickness in his hands. When it is cold, they move slowly and his gun medicine is weak."

Yomuli listened sympathetically as the priest explained that if the next day's weather remained damp and chill, McClain would probably die.

"And his death will be my fault, Yomuli. My sin."

Yomuli studied the priest's anguished face, placed a reassuring hand on his arm. "Priest find way. Always find way."

"Not this time. I have tried, but I can see no way. Even my prayers seem unanswered." Desperation showed in Miguel's eyes.

"Will of Heaven not help?" asked Yomuli uncertainly.

"In this, the will of Heaven is not clear to me."

The chief hesitated, then revealed diffidently that his tribe had an ancient remedy for stiffness of the limbs. It was a medicine of their old gods, passed down through the centuries to keep warriors nimble and diminish the sickness of age.

"It not from your Heaven, but much strong. Make sickness go. Make good medicine for gun-warrior."

Miguel stared at him, hope dawning on his

face. "This medicine . . . can it make the sickness go by morning?"

Yomuli nodded confidently. "Day come, no pain for gun-warrior. Hands go like arrow."

"Come, Yomuli. Your people must start making medicine at once."

As the two men strode briskly back toward the campfire, Yomuli remarked with a touch of pride, "Old gods sometimes smart like will of Heaven."

"In this instance, I think they *are* the will of Heaven," agreed Miguel gratefully.

Twenty-Five

Fed constantly by two braves, the campfire's flames climbed high and hot toward the night sky. McClain, stripped to the waist, lay sweating beside the fire on a bed of wet, steaming leaves. His arms were spread wide, and several warriors knelt on either side of him.

Scooping a thick greenish substance from scalding clay pots which nestled in the fire's coals, they massaged his torso, arms, and hands strongly.

Yomuli stood near McClain's head, chanting an ancient supplication to the tribal gods. Behind him, in a semicircle, several other braves beat hypnotic accompaniment on skin drums. Miguel hunkered beside McClain, watching the proceedings with lively interest.

The gunfighter bit back a groan as the warriors' brawny fingers kneaded his flesh and bones unceasingly.

"How long does this go on?" he gritted.

"Yomuli says it requires many hours," answered Miguel.

"Like hell!" McClain struggled to rise, but the warriors held him down firmly.

"Patience, my friend. To loosen your joints, the massage *must* be vigorous."

McClain choked on a whiff of steam. "Smell's worse than the pain. Feel like a scalded skunk."

"It is the herbs. They contain sulfur."

"If I can't shoot, maybe I can *stink* Peters t'death," McClain grumbled.

Miguel grinned, then asked eagerly, "Have your hands begun to tingle?"

"Everything tingles. Feel like I been struck by lightning."

Miguel's face lighted happily. "That is good! It indicates that the treatment is working!"

"Better work!" McClain coughed on another puff of steam.

"A little tingling is better than a bullet, my friend." Miguel returned the gunfighter's glare with a comforting smile.

In the chapel Lathrop and his companions sprawled uncomfortably among the wooden pews. All were hungry and ill-tempered, exchanging sour remarks and sarcastic accusations. From outside the Indians' drums and Yomuli's droning chant echoed maddeningly against the chapel walls.

Striding restlessly back and forth, Hal Peters

tried to ignore the sounds, without success. Suddenly his patience snapped. Crossing to the chapel doors, he jerked one open and fired a shot into the courtyard.

"Stop them damn drums!" he yelled.

An answering shot from the courtyard wall barely missed him. He jumped aside as Lathrop lunged forward and slammed the chapel doors.

"You loco, Peters? Suppose you'd been hit. We'd be in a helluva fix!"

"Can't stand Injun drums. Get me spooky!"

"All Injuns get *me* spooky," grumbled Hank.

"My old man used t'say the drums was bad luck," agreed Rafe nervously.

Lathrop turned on them angrily. "Shut up! All of you! They're just beatin' 'em t'*make* you spooky. It don't mean a thing. It's just noise!"

He crossed to a shelf at the side of the altar, pulled a bottle of sacramental wine from it, and handed it to Rafe.

"Here. Pass this around. It'll simmer you down!"

Rafe popped the cork sullenly, took a long swallow, and passed the wine to his nearest companion. Still sharing the bottle, the outlaws returned to seats in the various pews.

Twenty-Six

Hours later, when the warriors completed their ministrations to McClain, the cooking caldron, filled with water from the mission's spring, hung warming above the campfire.

The Indians washed the odorous salve from the gunfighter's body and covered him with a buffalo robe. A strange, heated oil was rubbed into his hands, which were then wrapped closely with skins. McClain felt sensuous warmth creeping through him. His limbs seemed flaccid, totally without tension or pain.

Now the drums and Yomuli's chanting stopped. The night fell silent, and McClain closed his eyes drowsily. When he opened them, a sunless dawn widened along the eastern horizon, forecasting another gray, chill morning.

Miguel and Yomuli sat vigil beside him. The other braves were scattered around the fire. All faces were turned anxiously toward the gunfighter. They brightened as he yawned and sat up, stretching effortlessly.

"How do you feel, my friend?" asked Miguel eagerly.

"Pretty good, I think." McClain stood carefully, stretched again, and flexed his fingers experimentally. Amazement flooded his features. "No pain at all! Fingers feel like they're lined with satin!"

The anxious faces relaxed, and a chorus of triumphant yells sounded from the warriors. Miguel clapped Yomuli on the back enthusiastically.

"Your medicine is strong, my brother! It will bring McClain victory!"

The gunfighter looked dubiously at the clouds hanging above the distant hills and rubbed his hands together. "Pretty chilly. Hope your medicine lasts till after the shootout, Chief."

Yomuli scooped a dipperful of hot, sweet-smelling liquid from a pot near the fire. "This more strong medicine. Secret from Old Ones. Make hands last. Give gun-warrior spirit magic."

"Spirit magic?" McClain turned to Miguel uneasily. "What's that mean?"

"It means the tribe looks upon this as a magic potion," smiled Miguel reassuringly.

"Potion? Suppose it makes me groggy?"

Miguel took a sip from the dipper, rolled it

in his mouth, then swallowed. "It is only a mixture of herbs and juices, McClain. Its effect is probably stimulating."

McClain accepted the dipper. "Hope the Old Ones knew what they were doin'!" He drank reluctantly, then returned the dipper to Yomuli.

The chief patted his shoulder encouragingly. "Old Ones know all, much wise."

The Indians watched McClain expectantly. After several moments, the gunfighter felt a surge of incredible energy. It throbbed through his veins, setting his body atingle and heightening all of his perceptions. The landscape, the distant hills, the faces around him, everything came into sharper focus.

Astonishment filled him. "I feel ten feet tall! Loose as a snake!"

Miguel and the Indians grinned with relief. Briskly confident, McClain pulled on his shirt and strapped his gun in place. On impulse, he drew the weapon, twirled it expertly, and returned it to its holster, his movements swift and fluid.

"I'll never get any quicker!" he exclaimed.

"Yomuli is right. The gods are with you, McClain. With *all* of us!" agreed Miguel happily.

Hal Peters's voice sounded loudly from the mission courtyard. "I'm waitin', McClain!

What's keepin' ya?"

The gunfighter turned and saw Peters standing arrogantly at the base of the chapel steps. Behind him, Lathrop and his men watched from the chapel doorway.

"Be right with you, Peters. Don't go way." McClain nodded tightly to his companions and strode forward to confront his challenger.

Miguel and the Indians followed. They ascended the courtyard walls to stand watching beside the guarding townsmen.

Peters swaggered to the center of the courtyard to meet McClain. They faced each other coldly, each measuring the other. Peters was smirkingly confident. McClain unreadable.

"It's past daylight, McClain. Thought you'd hightailed it."

"Just overslept," McClain retorted coolly.

"Where d'you want it? Belly . . . between the eyes? I don't mind accommodatin'."

The gunfighter remained undisturbed. "I'm not particular."

Peters smiled thinly. "Then start backin' up."

"Name the paces."

"Ten apiece. If y'can hit anything from that far."

"Your mouth's big enough t'hit from anyplace," responded McClain acidly.

As the two men backed away from each

other warily, each counting paces, the Indians began a slow, monotonous chant.

"Pipe them Injuns down!" yelled Peters edgily.

On the wall Miguel grinned wickedly and waved the braves to silence. Another wave and the chant was replaced by the beat of drums.

The sound increased Peters's irritation. "Goddamn it! Shut up!" he shouted.

The drumbeats softened, but continued. They sawed at Peters's nerves, turned his irritation to fury. At six paces, he lost control.

As the watchers gasped, he shrieked, "Damn all of ya!" His hand plunged to his gun. It came out blazing, leveled at McClain.

Instantly the gunfighter swung sideways. Peters's shot grazed his cheek as he fired from his holster. The bullet caught Peters in the chest and knocked him backward a step. He staggered, went loose-kneed, and sank to the ground. A bloody stain widened across his lifeless body, to become a dark pool on the sand.

For a moment those watching stood frozen, stunned into silence. Realization hit the outlaws first and brought sharp awareness of their defeat. They stormed from the chapel, crowded to the top of its steps, shouting that Miguel and the townspeople had tricked them again.

Miguel responded from the top of the wall. "You made a deal, *bandidos.* We will hold you to it!"

Lathrop glared up at him angrily. "You cheated, priest. Messed Peters up! Deal's off!"

"Peters was the cheat, *bandido.* He fired too soon."

"Deal's off, I say! *Off!*"

"You have lost, Lathrop. Accept it!" insisted Miguel firmly.

"No! McClain's the one should be dead!" Lathrop whirled toward the gunfighter, jerked out his gun.

McClain was too quick for him. Before Lathrop could fire, his weapon streaked from its holster, blazing as it cleared. The outlaw leader collapsed to the ground and lay still.

Before the other men could react, McClain swung his gun toward them. "You're licked, boys. Better face it," he advised grimly.

The outlaws looked from the gunfighter to the guns and spears covering them from the surrounding walls. Dismay grew on their features.

Rafe was the first to speak. "No sense dyin' for gold we can't get." He tossed his gun at McClain's feet.

"Smart thinkin'," McClain agreed. He looked at the others. "How about the rest of you?"

"I'll go along." Hank tossed his gun down beside Rafe's.

Sullenly the remaining outlaws threw their weapons on the pile. They stood waiting as the townsmen dropped from the walls and converged on them.

"You have made a wise choice," called Miguel. "Now you will take a trip instead of a bullet."

As the townsmen herded their prisoners to the rear of the courtyard, McClain crossed to Peters's body. Reaching down, he pulled his lucky piece from Peters's neck, wiped it with his neckerchief, and dropped it over his head, pleased to feel it dangling in its accustomed place.

He stood looking down at Peters for a moment. "Too bad the shamrock didn't bring *you* luck, fella."

Miguel spoke from behind him. "Stolen luck brings only disaster, my friend. That is the law of Heaven." He clapped McClain companionably on the shoulder.

Twenty-Seven

The morning was bright and warm, the sky sharply clear, and the air like wine. In the mission courtyard, Miguel, wearing his priest's robes, sat on a bench relating the story of David and Goliath to a circle of Indian children who listened raptly. Adult members of Yomuli's tribe moved about clearing the courtyard of debris and repairing the damaged chapel doors.

They chattered as they worked, their manner contented and happy. The old mission seemed to glow in response.

McClain rode into the courtyard and dismounted, taking in the pleasant scene with a smile. He tied his horse near the gateway and crossed to Miguel, who rose to greet him.

"Welcome, my friend. I wondered when you would come visiting." The priest's happiness matched the morning.

"Been busy in town. Had some decidin' t'do."

Miguel tapped the shiny new sheriff's badge

pinned to the gunfighter's chest. "I see that you have made a choice."

"Town needed a lawman. Asked me to take on the job." McClain's voice held a mixture of pride and self-consciousness.

"So you have found a resting place." Miguel's eyes twinkled knowingly. "A place for your 'itchy feet.' "

"I'll stick around awhile. Till they get itchy again."

"It is the will of Heaven, McClain. The town needs you, and so does its priest."

McClain was instantly suspicious. "What's a priest need with a lawman?"

"It is very simple." Miguel's tone was elaborately casual. "At times I must travel to remote towns where there is no other priest. The route is sometimes dangerous, and I need a little protection."

"A little protection, huh? Seems like I heard that someplace before."

Miguel's eyes were widely innocent. "I do not understand, my friend."

McClain grinned. "Hell, you don't! Devil's gonna get you someday, Padre!"

"Not if I see him coming!"

They burst into laughter.

Epilogue

In the mission courtyard, the old priest smiled at the tourist. "And that is the story of *'Padre Diablo',*" he concluded.

The visitor studied the swinging metal placard. "He was a brave man. The sign should say so."

The old priest chuckled. "He was also a tricky devil, and none were quite sure which was which. Are you?"

The visitor shook his head bewilderedly. "He was a strange priest. That's for sure."